Staying Pure

STEPHANIE PERRY MOORE

The Negro National Anthem

Lift every voice and sing
Till earth and heaven ring,
Ring with the harmonies of Liberty;
Let our rejoicing rise
High as the listening skies,
Let it resound loud as the rolling sea.
Sing a song full of the faith that the dark past has taught us,
Sing a song full of the hope that the present has brought us,
Facing the rising sun of our new day begun
Let us march on till victory is won.

So begins the Black National Anthem, written by James Weldon Johnson in 1900. Lift Every Voice is the name of the joint imprint of The Institute for Black Family Development and Moody Publishers.

Our vision is to advance the cause of Christ through publishing African-American Christians who educate, edify, and disciple Christians in the church community through quality books written for African Americans.

Since 1988, the Institute for Black Family Development, a 501(c)(3) nonprofit Christian organization, has been providing training and technical assistance for churches and Christian organizations. The Institute for Black Family Development's goal is to become a premier trainer in leadership development, management, and strategic planning for pastors, ministers, volunteers, executives, and key staff members of churches and Christian organizations. To learn more about The Institute for Black Family Development, write us at:

The Institute for Black Family Development
15151 Faust
Detroit, MI 48223

We hope you enjoy this book from Moody Publishers. Our goal is to provide high-quality, thought-provoking books and products that connect truth to your real needs and challenges. For more information on other books and products written and produced from a biblical perspective, go to www.moodypublishers.com or write to:

Moody Publishers/LEV
820 N. LaSalle Boulevard
Chicago, IL 60610
www.moodypublishers.com

Staying Pure

STEPHANIE PERRY MOORE

ISBN-10: 0-8024-4236-6
ISBN-13: 978-0-8024-4236-9

10

Printed in the United States of America

To my precious daughter
SYDNI DEREK
whose newborn innocence
allowed me to filter out,
through the written word,
what purity is!

Contents

Acknowledgments

*A*s I get ready for my ten-year class reunion, I remember some of my favorite high school friends. Like Payton Skky, the main character in this book, I also remember some favorite classes. Like Chemistry.

Chemistry is an interesting class. In order to test a given substance, you need certain tools. And you need to strain it—strain out everything that is *NOT* the substance—in order to find out what it really is.

The same was true for the writing of this book. Here is a special thank you to all who aided in its creation.

To my parents, Franklin and Shirley Perry: You are like my *BEAKER.* You two have held the substance of my dreams close to your hearts for years. Without your love, nurture, and support, I would have never had the courage to realize my goals. Straining out my character—discovering who I really am—has caused me to be and write who I am.

To my personal editor, Marla Clark, my mentor, Matthew Parker, and to the folks at Moody: You all are my *MIXER.* With the absence of your stirring up the best from my work, my solution (or should I say, book) would have never been ready to be poured onto the shelves. Even though the road to getting me published was tough, your belief in me and my project made you work until I was signed. Straining my written thoughts has created a book of which we can both be extremely proud.

To my reading pool, Jacci Dixon, Virgi Johnson, Barbie Jones, Launi Perriman, and Cole Smith: You all are my *PETRI DISH.* After mixing up each chapter, your open hands were there for me to place the bare essence of this manuscript. Thanks for holding together truth and helping me discern what needed to go.

To my husband, Derrick Moore: You are my *BUNSEN BURNER.* Not only do you heat up my life with your love, but you also allow my passion for God to burn strong. If you had not stayed on me and melted down my procrastination, then this book would still be unfinished. Straining my impure soul with God's Word has enabled me to become a better writer, friend, mother, and wife.

To the reader, wherever you are: You are the WATER. Every word in this book was meant to flow through your soul. As you pour over each page, may your hearts be receptive to the words, and to the Word you hear from God as well.

And to my Lord, Jesus Christ: You are the SALT! Without You, nothing in me could be pure. Thanks for giving me the vision and outlet to share my life's lessons in a positive fashion. Straining my sin has given me the desire to live my life to please You and encourage others. May we all see Your light and not strain, but strive, to follow such purity!

1

Driving
from "No!"

"N o!" I shouted at the top of my voice. "Stop, Dakari. Please stop!"

He kept on kissing me as if he'd heard me say "yes" instead of "no."

"I mean it!" I yelled as I pushed him back over to the driver's side of the car.

Dakari voiced in anger, "What's your problem? I thought you wanted this as much as me. I took all this time to plan . . ."

"Plan what?" I cut in with disgust. "We're at a rest stop in my jeep, parked beside a beat-up truck with a German Shepherd tied to the back of it, barking loudly, on the way to your brother's college football game. I mean, really Dakari, how much of this did you actually plan?"

As I talked, I was busy buttoning my pants. My boyfriend of two years was doing the same. However, it was more than clear he was furious that I had stopped our ten minutes of passion. My roomy jeep was all out of space that day.

"Dannng . . . Payton, I thought you wanted this. I thought you wanted me. We've been dating now ever since we were in the tenth grade. It's my senior year and . . . well . . . I must say that I need more from our relationship. This is unacceptable," he stated with a stern voice as he started the car.

Tears rolled down my caramel cheeks as he began driving again. *Unacceptable,* I thought deeply to myself. How could he say that to me with such seriousness? Did he think that all we had could be easily thrown away if sex didn't enter the picture? Was he threatening to leave me if I did not give in?

Shoot, don't get me wrong; I love him. Not only have I liked him since I was in the seventh grade, but so has every other girl in our school—no, our city. Well, except for my three friends, that is. They love and respect me too much to even think of messing with Dakari. Plus, they all have boyfriends of their own.

Why such an attraction to my guy, Dakari Ross Graham? That's easy. If you could see him, you'd think he was Denzel Washington's younger brother. A 6'0", 185-pound toned body, with perfect honey brown skin, wavy hair, 20/20 vision, and a beautiful smile. What more could any girl want her guy to look like? But if that isn't enough to attract your attention, he is also the most popular boy in our large high school, since he is the star of our football team. On top of that, he's an honor student.

That's why everyone thinks we're the hottest couple around. I'm the cheerleading captain, president of the honor society, vice president of the Student Government Association, senior editor of our newspaper staff, and a debutante.

Actually, I'm quite looking forward to early April when the civic organization, The Links Incorporated, presents fifty seniors from the metropolitan area to our city in a coming out ball. At first, I didn't know if I'd get selected. After

11

all, one hundred fifty-six girls submitted applications to be chosen as a part of this elite group. It's such a big deal in our town. Most of my friends said I was a shoe in, not because of my accomplishments, but because my mother has been a member of the Links organization for twelve years now. However, my mom told me not to assume anything. I didn't know I'd made it until I got a letter of acceptance in the mail—just like everyone else.

Well, we'd been driving for about twenty-five miles, and neither of us had said a word. We'd just been listening to the radio. Truthfully, I couldn't believe he was acting like this. It's not as though this was the first time I'd said, "No!" We had come close many times before, unfortunately, but he'd always said he understood.

I am a virgin, and I want to stay that way till I'm married. My belief in God is what makes my head feel this way. I know that God calls us to wait. It's just my heart that I'm having trouble with. My feelings are so strong for Dakari that I feel like a popsicle on a hot summer day. I melt!

So that's my struggle. I don't lead Dakari on intentionally. Cause when I'm in his arms, I want him just as much as he wants me. But so far, I've always seemed to realize that God would not be pleased. So I stop. Could you imagine God frowning on you from heaven? Not the nicest image.

"So are you gonna talk to me, or what?" I asked in a pitiful voice, sounding like a baby calling for its mother.

"Got nothin' to say," Dakari stated, obviously annoyed with me. "I'm just trying to get us to the game without an argument. Please do not start one."

All I could do was look out the window, up to the sky. It was such a lovely day—too beautiful to be down. The end of August in Georgia is usually very hot. Since we'd had rain the past few days, the atmosphere had cooled down. It was seventy-four degrees, and not a cloud to be found. A great day for Southern Conference football.

Dakari's older brother, Drake, was really good at football. He was a senior at the University of Georgia. At 6'1", two hundred thirty-one pounds, this inside linebacker was the top candidate for the Dick Butkus award going into the season. That's the highest honor given to an NCAA division 1A defensive linebacker. From what I heard, a lot of NFL scouts would be at this game to check out his performance.

Dakari truly admires his brother. Sometimes it makes me sick to see how much pressure he puts on himself to be like Drake, or to exceed what his brother has done.

The game was not only just about Drake. Dakari had special interest in it as well. He was being recruited by Georgia since he was projected to have a thousand-yard rushing season. And because Athens is only an hour and a half away from Augusta, Dakari is really considering them as his first choice. It doesn't hurt that Drake goes there too. But he also likes Auburn. I guess it's because Bo Jackson, Dakari's all-time favorite player, played there. He always says, "Bo is the greatest athlete of our lifetime!" I'm not that into sports, so I wouldn't know. I just yell and scream, especially when my boyfriend carries the ball.

This was the first of two visits that the University of Georgia had set up for Dakari. He got to bring his parents and a guest to tour the athletic facilities, have lunch, and watch the game. Then sometime later this fall, Dakari was invited for an overnight visit. That's when he'll meet the head coach, hang out with the players, visit a guidance counselor, and tour the entire campus.

We were meeting his parents up there. They left early that morning so they could have breakfast with Drake. I thought that was weird, since Drake had to play a game against Tennessee. But Dakari informed me that the players get to report late since it is a four o'clock game.

As we exited off the interstate, I just felt uneasy. I didn't want to be around Dakari's folks when it was clear we were having problems. Nor did I want Dakari to be so mad at me that everyone would notice his negative attitude. So, I tried again to break the ice. This time, however, before I spoke, I prayed.

Silently I thought, "Lord, I'm struggling bad in the area of fornication. But You know me. Even when I let You down, I still plead for Your help. Father, only You know that I'm trying really hard to stay pure. After all, I did finally say, 'No!' even if it was after I almost had my clothes off. Fortunately, Lord, I did stop. I just need Your continued strength in this area. But now I ask You to fill me with the right words to say. I love Dakari and I just want him to open up and . . . well . . . basically get over it! Please help me. Please, dear Lord, help us."

After hesitating, I softly spoke, "Dakari, I know you're upset. And you should be. I did get you as worked up as you got me. But we both made a commitment long ago to wait . . . and I want to stick to it. Don't be mad at me for wanting to honor God. I mean, it's not like I stopped because I don't love you."

Looking over at him, I could tell my words were sinking in. His whole demeanor had changed. He didn't appear to be so uptight.

Noticing his pleasant change, I took the liberty of making a statement that I knew he would love to hear. "Sweetie, you know I want you to be my first," I expressed tenderly.

"Yeah, I thought you did," Dakari voiced in a teddy bear tone.

I replied, "I just want to make sure you're my only. Remember, I love you that much!"

"And, Payton, I love you too! It's just getting hard. What can I say? Shoot, I'm a growing man and my needs are changing. I am trying to keep them in check. But when you rub me like that and say those things you whisper in my ear . . . the way you say them, I can't control anything," he said woundedly.

From that point, until we parked, I felt we really connected. He's honest with me and I appreciate that. I just feel glad that he is able to let out his feelings. And I mine. 'Cause I learned a long time ago that keeping things all bottled up only makes for a super big explosion sooner or later.

This seems weird. All these college women dressed in uniforms practically flirting with these young high school boys. If another one comes prancing over here to my man, I'm gonna—

"Oh my gosh, you're Dakari Graham, Drake's little brother. I've been waiting all morning to meet you," this absolutely gorgeous girl said, fawning over my guy.

She interrupted my thought.

"I'm Shari Rice. You're my recruit!" she blabbed excitedly. "Why don't I give you and Mr. Graham a tour. I know you both have probably seen everything. After all, our best defensive player, number fifty-five, is your relative. However, we have several new things that Coach Eckerd has added this season. And you absolutely must see them."

Mr. Graham responded, "Sure, we'd love to check them out."

Dakari smiled continually at this Shari girl and just nodded his nappy head as to give his approval of her idea. He practically drooled, obviously ecstatic that she was his hostess. Mrs. Graham and I just stood together on the other side of her. Shari then turned to us and stared. I'd swear, if I were of the betting kind, she was sizing me up.

"Well, I'm sure your lovely mother and adorable little sister want to stay here in the recruiting room," she said confidently, as if I could be nothing more.

I walked around her and discreetly tried to tap Dakari so he'd speak up. But I saw his mother chuckle out of the corner of my eye. She and I have been tight for years. It seemed that Mrs. Graham always had my back.

"Oh, that's not his sister, honey," his mother voiced with pride.

Dakari came out of his daze and said, "Uh—no, this is my girlfriend, Payton!"

"Pay-ton," Shari uttered almost sarcastically while she extended her clay-colored hand. "It's nice to meet you. Wow, you must be the luckiest girl in your school."

"Shoot, no ma'am! He's the lucky one. Not only is she smart, but her daddy is rich," Mr. Graham said jokingly.

Frankly, I don't know why everyone always assumes that we're rich. My father is the first and only black automobile dealer in town. He owns a Chrysler dealership that he inherited from his dad, who founded the CBDA, Chrysler Black Dealer Association. Though my grandpa is still alive, he retired and moved to Conyers, Georgia, with my grandmother. We have money and all, but my dad—whose word to me is as good as the Bible—tells me "by no means are we rich." We do live in the nicest neighborhood in town, however, and I count it a blessing that I have never wanted a thing I didn't get.

As the three of them walked away I asked, "Mrs. Graham, who are these girls?"

The two of us sat at a nearby table and she replied, "Oh, they are called Georgia Girls. They're the official hostesses for the football team. The university uses them to help entice these boys to their school. If I'm not mistaken, almost every major division one school has some similar organization. The majority of these girls do a classy job, but it's clear that all do not. Miss Shari has another agenda. She's a bit too . . . friendly. Actually, I thought Drake's girlfriend, Hayli, would be Dakari's hostess. She is an officer in this group."

Mrs. Graham loved to see her boys dating successful women. She is an accountant, on the board of trustees at her church, and treasurer of the Delta Sigma Theta Alumnae chapter, of which my mom is also a member.

"You've met her, right Payton?" she questioned while stretching her neck to look around for Hayli.

"Yes ma'am," I answered, "at your home this summer, for your Fourth of July picnic. We really didn't get a chance to chat, but she seemed nice."

"I like her a lot. She wants to be a dentist and hopefully have her own practice. Plus, she's always there for my baby! I've ruled out the fact that she is only with him because of his success. Mr. Graham and I met her parents at a game last year and they were very sweet people. She only has one flaw," Mrs. Graham stated with a smiling frown on her face.

I asked, "What's that?"

"She's an AKA," his mother blurted out.

I haven't quite understood the rivalry between the Deltas and the Alpha Kappa Alpha sorority. I've asked my mother about it, and she said I'll understand it better when and if I pledge myself.

My friend Dymond has an older sister who goes to South Carolina State University. Well, she was trying to pledge one of the sororities, but they wouldn't accept her. They heard that she had gone to the other sorority's rush. Having different black female organizations is great, but not when we get so involved with stupid stuff that we tear each other down.

An hour passed and neither Dakari, his father, nor Shari was back. The game would be starting soon. I caught myself getting paranoid. *What if he wants to date his pretty hostess? How will he break it to me?* I shook my head. *No, that can't be the case. Our love is too strong,* I told myself to ease my worry.

Mrs. Graham had gone to the washroom. When she returned, Hayli was with her. It does feel good to be starting my last year of high school, but I imagine Hayli has got to be on top of the world. A senior in college! That's impressive! I just pray God grants me the opportunity to feel the same joy one day.

"Look who I ran into in the ladies' room," Mrs. Graham stated with enthusiasm. "Hayli, you remember Payton, Dakari's friend? Well, she's joining us this visit."

Hayli smiled at me and asked, "How've you been?"

"I'm great! Thanks for asking. And you?" I questioned.

"Things are going pretty good. I was telling Mrs. Graham that she doesn't have to worry about our hostess Shari coming on to her younger son," Hayli commented.

I quickly said with a disturbed tone, "How can you be so sure?"

"Well, ask anyone here and they'll tell you. Shari is after Drake. She's always going to the dorm, leaving notes on his car. That daggone girl sent him flowers last week on the first day of school. She's just hoping Dakari and Mr. Graham will put in a good word for her," she uttered with disgust in her voice.

The three of us kept talking about how scandalous some women can be when they decide they want someone else's man. I didn't believe we were gossiping because we really weren't referring to anyone in particular. Although, over the two years that I've dated Dakari, I've had my share of run-ins with girls thinking they could just up and take my guy.

I guess you could say that for the rest of the game, Hayli became the hostess for Mrs. Graham and me. Dakari took it upon himself to sit beside Shari the whole game. He's got some nerve. The boy didn't even ask me if it was OK with me. However, since they were sitting two rows in front of us, I was able to make sure things stayed on the up-and-up between Shari and him.

18

At halftime Dakari's family seemed to be extremely pleased. Drake had two sacks and a forced fumble. The team was also ahead of Tennessee by twenty-one points. All of the recruits were on the field, watching as the guys warmed up. Some of the special recruits got to go in the locker room. Dakari was one of the chosen few. Hayli said if they are picked to go in at the break, then the coach really wants to make a good impression.

During the middle of the third quarter, Dakari came back to our section. He came straight over to where I was sitting with Hayli and his parents and introduced this really cute guy.

"Hey, everyone! Meet my newfound friend, Tad Taylor. He was in the locker room with me," Dakari announced with a fake smile.

Mr. Graham responded in an investigating tone, "Tad Taylor? Ahh, this is North Augusta's star halfback. Son, this is your competition, when it comes to stats and all. Say, Tad, how many yards are you planning on running this year?"

"Oh, sir, I don't honestly know. Whatever God allows me to get will be just fine with me," Tad answered humbly.

Dakari didn't like this guy. It was obvious even when he was introducing us to Tad that he practically despised him. This Morris Chestnut look-alike's Worchestershire Sauce-colored skin and short Schwarzenegger body made him almost irresistible. But when Dakari introduced me as his lady, neither he nor I expected the enticing response we got from Tad. When I reached out my hand to shake his, this intriguing gentleman took my fingers gently and kissed them.

Wow! I absolutely thought that I'd faint into his arms. If my heart did not belong to Dakari, I probably would have. And if my boyfriend looked any madder, steam would have been shooting out his ears. I was glad to know that my man could still get jealous.

As I lay in the passenger seat of my Chrysler Jeep, I just relaxed. It had been such a trying day. My sunroof was open and I reclined in the seat, adoring the starry night. Dakari and Drake had gone for a stroll so that they could catch up on things. I told him I'd meet him at the car.

While I waited, I looked past the stars and focused on the God I could clearly see in the clouds.

"Lord," I began in a quiet voice, "school is gonna start in two days, and I have no idea what to expect out of my senior year. Actually, I'm a little frightened. What if my grades slip? I'm registered for all these AP classes. I'm told that the teachers on that level are horrible. Help me to impress them. Oh, and my friends . . . Father, I don't want to fall out with them. Let us get along. Only You know how bossy Dymond can be, or how whiney Rain always is, and how insensitive Lynzi seems. OK, OK, Holy Spirit, I confess. I'm not the greatest friend either. I'm working on that. And I know I've asked You to bless my relationship with Dakari ten thousand times, but please . . . I come once again asking You to keep us together."

About five minutes later, I heard Dakari and Drake coming to the car. They couldn't see me because I was reclining. Just as I started to raise up and speak to them, I was frozen by words that numbed my soul.

"I don't know, Drake, man," Dakari stated with concern. "My thing with Payton is getting a little old. I do love her and all, but . . ."

Drake cut in and said, "You want to have sex with her?"

"Heck yes! I do. I mean, dang, we've been dating for two whole years."

I was disappointed.

He continued, "I've played along with this 'wait till we're married' stuff for long enough. Shoot, she knows I'm there for her. This is just unacceptable."

There it was again. The phrase that put a lump in my

throat. "Lord," I pondered, speaking in a whisper to the sky. "What are You doing up there? I just finished praying. Didn't You hear me? I asked You to keep us together. Yet as I listen—eavesdrop, actually—it sounds as if we're headed apart, unless I GIVE IN! Lord, is that what You want? Only You know how much I love him. It feels as if I'm being pushed into a corner. One kiss from Dakari, and they might as well hand me a cream-colored wedding dress. What else do I do with this information but give in? I can't lose him, Lord. Or can I? No, no, I can't."

After my talk with God, I closed the sunroof and rolled down the window. Dakari and Drake looked surprised. "Hey guys," I said, looking tired.

"Payton, we didn't know you were in there. What were you doing all this time?" Drake asked, obviously picking me to see if I had heard them.

"Oh, I was just dozing," I stated, sort of stretching the truth.

They said their goodbyes, and I hugged Drake. I wanted to go off on them both. I wanted them to tell me to my face what they discussed behind my back. However, I retreated in silence. Our ride home was much the same as the drive up. We hardly said a thing. I told Dakari I was sleepy, so I wouldn't have to pretend. Frankly, at that point I was all confused. If Dakari loved me the way that I loved him, then how could he say what he said? All the way home I tried to answer that question. But when we got to Augusta, I still didn't have an answer. All I knew was that our relationship was dramatically different, ever since we started driving from NO!

2

Controling My Man

"So, have you guys heard?" Lynzi asked with excitement as she entered the backseat of my car.

"Oh, no you don't, Miss Thang," I responded, looking at my girlfriend as if she had lost her mind. "How dare you enter my ride and not even say 'Hello' or 'Good morning' to me and Rain. Don't nobody wanna hear no gossip."

Rain's quiet voice contradicted me, "Speak for yourself, Payton. I wanna hear the latest."

"All you two can think to talk about is other people," I said with an attitude.

"Well, excuse me," Lynzi teased. "What's wrong with you?"

"She was like that when I got in the car . . . and all I said was 'Hello,'" Rain commented. "Maybe we should just catch the bus to school, Lynzi."

"Well, I don't know 'bout all that," Lynzi quickly replied, looking over the seat directly at Rain. "No, seriously Payton, what's wrong?"

I didn't know whether to tell my best friends or keep this to myself. The fact was, Dakari and I were having severe problems. If our relationship was a burn, it would now be considered . . . "third degree." Yesterday, he didn't call me at all. For us, that was a definite sign of trouble. If we didn't speak at least three times a day something was wrong. But not speaking at all! I was really buggin.'

Besides pacing the floor waiting for him to ring my phone, I had tried on fourteen outfits deciding what to wear the first day of school. He always liked it when I wore my form-fitting black jeans. So, to catch his eye, I decided to wear them.

That's what I was thinking about: could I win back his attention? When Lynzi snapped me back with, "Hello . . . earth to Payton."

I turned from my silence and said with watery eyes, "Dakari and I aren't doing that good."

Rain spoke with concern, "Payton, what do you mean? You guys are tighter than tight. What could possibly happen to shake you two up?"

"It's hard to explain. Well, not really," I said reluctantly. "Basically, he wants to sleep with me, and I don't know if I can. As it is, my resistance has caused major tension. I'm afraid if I don't, we're through."

"Maybe, then, that's best. Is he really worth not sticking to your commitment?" Rain insisted, as if I should say no!

Lynzi responded before I could answer, "Oh, yeah. Hot, fine Dakari Graham is worth it. Girlfriend, loosen up and let him set you on fire!"

We entered the school parking lot as the two of them bickered back and forth. I knew not to solicit their opinions. It was evident that they were biased. Rain had not been intimate with a guy. If she had her way, she'd be my personal gatekeeper to assure no man enters until I say, "I do!" Lynzi, on the other hand, cannot wait for the day that

23

I open up physically to a guy. She acts like hearing that I'm no longer a virgin will somehow ease her guilt. Lynzi once told me when she was tipsy from a wine cooler she had snagged from her mother's stash, "Sometimes I hate that my innocence is lost."

As we got out of the car, our girlfriend Dymond ran toward us. She is the sexiest one-hundred-sixty-pound woman I had ever seen . . . with her short skirts and beautiful smooth skin. Her hair is as silky and reddish brown as my grandmother's cow Bessie.

"So Lynzi," Dymond said, out of breath, "Did you tell them?"

Lynzi looked at me and said, "Something else came up."

"What's the big news?" I asked impatiently.

We headed inside the school and Dymond explained, "There's this new girl. And from what I saw last night, we all better grab tighter to our men 'cause this chick has her claws sharp."

"What did you see last night?" Rain asked with desperation in her voice.

Dymond huddled us together and said, "I went to the movies with my cousin from Beech Island, right? And, well, afterwards we went to Howard James Barbecue to eat. I don't know why ya'll weren't there. The place was packed."

Howard James Barbecue is a little hole in the wall that serves the best pork and hash you'd ever wanna taste. It's been the hangout spot for a while now. Not only is the food good, but the dark atmosphere with pool and other games in every corner keeps the owner Howard and his wife Gussie Bell very busy.

Dymond continued, "Anyway, things were as they always are. You know, some guys smacking and some guys macking. Basically, everybody was doing their own thing. Then all of a sudden, this high yellow Robin Givens wanna-be walked in wearing a tight—too tight—white leather pantsuit. Now ya'll know it was eighty-two degrees last night. However—"

"Excuse me, Dymond," Rain cut in with annoyance in her voice, "I'm high yellow! You say it as if it's a bad thing. I can't help it if you are—"

Dymond broke her off and calmly said, "See, now why you trippin'? My mama always told me that nice lighter skinned folks were referred to as light skinned, but the ones who think they are all that are called high yellow. This chick that walked into our hangout place, swinging her hair and hips at the same time, most definitely thought that she was all that. Every guy's eye in the place was on her. Including Fatz! And you know I was ticked, 'cause that's my man."

"Well, what else do you know about her?" I questioned.

"See, that's just it," Dymond interjected. "Me and my cousin left shortly after that. Shoot, I had to take her home, and that was a twenty-five minute ride one way. I hated leaving. Our crew of fellas seemed to want to be all over her. But I made Fatz promise he'd call me in an hour. Since he was driving Dakari, Bam, and Tyson home, I felt good, you know, since the finest guys in the place would be gone."

"How do you know she's going to school here." I asked, hoping Dymond was wrong earlier.

"Because, girl, Fatz told me when he called last night. Oh yeah, and guess what her name is: Starr Love! Do you believe that?"

"That name sounds like trouble," Lynzi said.

On the first day of school, there is always an assembly for the seniors, a time where our cool principal, Dr. Franklin, gives us a pep talk. Our class of one hundred twenty-one predominantly African-American students were all in the gym. I admit we were a tad juvenile at first— throwing pieces of paper at each other and yelling across the open space. But when the head man walked in, we all calmed down. He sure had our respect.

"So they let anybody become seniors, huh?" Dr. Franklin stated in a joking way. "Seriously though, I'm extremely proud of each and every one of you. Remember, you are the first class that will graduate under my full administration. We all started here together and have been through several changes. Fortunately, you've hung in there and are on the last leg. Don't mess up. I'm counting on you guys to set the example for the underclassmen. It's been said that most of you won't graduate . . . Let's prove them wrong."

As he talked, I looked around for Dakari. I couldn't believe I hadn't seen him. Dymond was sitting by me and she kept saying that she had something to tell me through the assembly. Lynzi and Rain were sitting on the other side of me. We had to sit with our first period class. Dymond and I were excited to learn that our first four classes were together. They were all honor courses.

Every time Dymond fixed her lips to tell me whatever it was this time, Mrs. Guice, our AP calculus teacher, would hush her up. It felt like I was at the ophthalmologist's office reading a chart the way my eyes were scanning the bleachers. It was odd that I couldn't find my boyfriend.

I'm not trying to brag or nothing, but I'm a pretty good-looking gal. Five feet five inches tall and one hundred twenty-five pounds. With honey brown skin, I turn a few heads. Actually, I've only been at school for an hour and a few gentlemen have already inquired about a date. Well, one was a freshman, so I won't count him.

"Before I let you go," I heard Dr. Franklin say as I briefly tuned back into him, "just remember that only you can control what happens to you this year. Don't look back and regret your decisions. Make wise choices now. If you need me, I've got plenty of room in my office at the front of the school. Now kids, get out of here and get some knowledge into those brains. And hey, let's have a great year!"

Just as we all rose to exit the gymnasium and go to our respective classes, the bell rang. It was like that sound woke my brain up. Next, I immediately spotted the love of my life.

"Girl, there he is," I said excitedly to Dymond as I pointed to Dakari heading out the door. "You know I love—"

Before I could finish that statement, I saw the most horrific, unbelievably confusing sight. This girl whom I had never seen had *her* arm around *my* man's waist. They were laughing. I thought I'd faint when I saw him return her gesture, placing his arm around her. My mouth hung open, as I flopped down on the nearest bench.

My true friend spoke to comfort me. "Payton, I know you're hurting. I'm not sure of everything that's going on with you and Dakari, but it's obvious that things aren't all together. I was trying to tell you earlier that Fatz told me he didn't take Dakari home last night. It seems Mr. 'No Good' Graham rode home with Starr," she said in a most sympathetic voice.

"Are you serious, Dy?" I asked with a teary heart.

Dymond responded, "Yeah, and unfortunately, Fatz thinks he likes this girl."

"Was that her?" I questioned, still not believing this whole thing. "Was that this Moon person?"

"Starr is her name, Payton. Not Moon," Dymond said as she just had to correct me. "That was her."

By this time, my sadness had turned to anger. "Shoot, moon, cloud, sun, star—I don't care. But I'm going after them. I have to get to the bottom of this."

I jumped to my feet, grabbed my black bag, and raced to the door.

"Wait for me!" Dymond screamed from a distance.

When I got outside the gym, they were nowhere to be found. I searched and searched through the crowded hallway, but still had no luck. As I turned down the science hall, I heard a big commotion. It seemed that someone else had beat me to the punch of confronting Dakari.

All I could hear was Dakari's voice saying, "You better step off. It's none of your business."

I actually thought it was one of my girlfriends taking up for me. I mean, here it is, Dakari and I weren't even broken up. Well, if we were, I wasn't told about it. And here he is being seen around a school that I've run for three years, in the arms of another. Yet, when I got to the middle of the circle, I was surprised to find my younger brother, Perry, defending my honor.

"How you gonna diss my sister like that man?" Perry yelled as he pushed Dakari on the shoulder, throwing him back a few feet.

I screamed, "Perry, no!"

Luckily, I got there when I did because they were about to fight. My brother may only be a sophomore, but he's tough. Dakari had much respect for Perry and vice versa. They are even teammates. Last year, my little brother, a wide receiver, was the only freshman to start on the team. They had been in football camp all summer long and had developed quite a good rapport. Shoot, they have a lot in common: both offensive players, and both love me. But at that moment the tension was so thick, you couldn't chop it with an axe.

"Guys, let's not get worked up," I said, standing between them.

"Who is SHE, Kari?" Starr asked, placing her well-manicured hand on Dakari's chest.

I grabbed hers and flung it off his chest.

"KARI!" I said as I stared him in the face, "the question is, who is she?"

Starr blabbed, "Don't—don't touch me again."

"I won't have to, as long as you don't overstep and touch my man," I said.

"Oh," Starr said with her eyes wide as if a secret had been told. "This is the ex-girlfriend that you said couldn't satisfy you?"

"Ex?" I asked hesitantly, hoping that she didn't know something I didn't, nor did I want to.

Starr spoke in a sly tone, "Yes honey, I assume he became my man when I gave what you wouldn't, or should I say couldn't, last night!"

My focus had been so channeled to Dakari and this bimbo that I had forgotten the audience. Well, after that comment, the folks reminded me of their presence. All the hissing and ooohing got on my nerves. I was both stunned and embarrassed at the same time. Trying to hold it together in front of the crowd, I turned away from Dakari and Starr, excusing my way through the crowd. The bell rang again and everyone jetted to second period.

When I was clear of the masses, I ran to a corner under the stairs and cried. I don't know how long I was in that state. I do know that I've never felt so empty.

"Payton Skky, is that you under those steps?" I heard an authoritative voice shout.

Trying to talk and dry my eyes at the same time, I said, "Yes sir!"

It was Dr. Franklin. He made me go with him to his office. Our principal looked out for me. My friends said he treats me special because my father is on the school board. That probably is true, yet he always relates to me as a genuine mentor and friend.

Dr. Franklin's office was pretty elaborate. The darn thing is larger than our largest classroom. He has plaques all over the wall. Rumor has it that he's up for the Augusta school system superintendent's job. It's becoming available at the end of the school year. Right now we've got an interim boss because this summer Dr. Pugh, who held the position for eight years, pleaded guilty to embezzling school funds.

"So, what's the problem?" Dr. Franklin kindly asked, as he handed me a glass of water and a tissue. He isn't the nicest looking fifty-year-old man. Short and stocky, he has a belly like a bowl full of jelly, plump and giggly. He'd put you in the mind of a black Colonel Sanders. You know, Colonel Sanders, the chicken man.

Everyday for the last three years, he wore a black suit. When I was a freshman, I thought it was the same ugly polyester suit. One day, a bunch of us finally got the nerve to ask him. I still remember his response. The man is so crazy.

"The same suit?" Dr. Franklin said laughingly, "You guys must be crazy. Or heck, you all must think I am. Shucks, I got a job. I work Monday through Friday. Remember, I am not tight. Everyday someone is begging me for money. 'Dr. Franklin, can I have a dollar?' 'Ah, sir, loan me fifty cents.' Sound familiar? Just to kill your curiosity, I have twenty black suits. Hey, what can I say, I look good in black."

We all laughed for days. Most of us still tease him occasionally. We say, "Ooh Dr. Franklin, you sure look goooood in black!" Actually, when he's about to give a demerit or something, nine times out of ten, if we give him that compliment, we get off scot-free.

Finally, after being embarrassed, I opened up and told my principal everything. It felt natural. He is just that easy to talk to.

"Girl, you're crazy letting that tackhead joker get to you. With all the stuff you have on the ball, I wouldn't give losing him a second thought. Now, I'm going to tell you something, and if you are smart, you'll take this advice seriously," Dr. Franklin voiced as he leaned over his desk and looked me straight in the eye. "If you really feel that Dakari Graham is the one and only, and you can't live without him etc., etc., ignore him. He'll come back. On the other hand, Payton, if you go around here moping, crying, begging, and caring, he'll run as fast as he can in the opposite direction. And remember, if he doesn't come back, you will be better off without him."

We talked a little while longer. I really felt better after our discussion. Dr. Franklin had convinced me to be strong. When he saw a slight smile on my face, he wrote me a pass.

As I walked out the door, he kidded, "Don't worry about paying me monetarily for this counseling session. It was free. I do, however, expect to be paid by seeing the name Payton Skky on my straight-A honor roll."

After taking a positive attitude, the day just flew by. It was already seventh period: cheerleading for me. Well, really it's called Athletics. I think it's so cool that we get a grade for yelling and screaming. It works out great. Not only is it good because the football team is nearby, but if we get our formation, routines, stunts, and cheers down, we don't have to stay after school for practice.

Lynzi is my only tight girlfriend on the squad. Dymond is on flag corps. We got mad when she didn't make the dance team. Word got out that the judges thought she was too fat and kept her off. And supposedly, she was the best one that tried out. Now Rain is on the girls' basketball team. She's the most feminine, cutest player I've ever seen. Rain sits out when she breaks a nail, but she can ball.

As I came out of the locker room from changing into my shorts, I noticed Dakari doing warm-ups. I quickly turned and walked the other way. The only class we have together is second period Physics with Ms. Brown. However, I missed that class today due to my session in the office. Therefore, I hadn't seen the chump since that girl informed me that my man was no longer my man.

I truly thought he'd let me go my own way. You see, Dakari hates scenes. But before I could get too far away, he jumped in front of me.

Out of breath, he gasped, "Payton, we need to talk."

"Dakari, or should I say KARI," I sighed in a smart tone, "I can't deal with this now. So please get out of my way."

He responded, "No, I don't wanna talk here. I was thinking maybe I could come by and swoop you up after my practice."

"Well, if I'm there and I feel like it . . . then maybe," I stated, giving him the hard time that he so richly deserved.

"Come on, baby. Please don't play me like this. My heart is breaking and I wanna straighten things," he explained with a grin on his adorable face.

I was so happy to hear him say that he wanted to work things out. But could I really forgive all this stuff? *Maybe it's not all true. I haven't spoken to Dakari. Yeah, that's it. Starr lied,* I pondered.

Immediately, I fell back into love. "Sure, we can get together!" I exclaimed with excitement. "I'll be ready."

Dakari hugged me and said, "Cool!"

When cheerleading practice was over, Lynzi and I sat in my car while we waited for Rain to come out of the locker room. We thought her team would be finished when we were, but they were running over. I didn't want to wait all day because I needed to get home and change. I was ecstatic that Dakari and I were gonna work things out. Truthfully, I couldn't believe I fell for all that garbage Starr told me anyway. You'd think I would have more faith in my guy.

Lynzi nosily asked, "So, before practice I saw you and Dakari locked in an embrace. What's all that about?"

"What do you mean, 'What's that all about?' That's a dumb question, Lynzi. He's my darn boyfriend; that's what it's about," I said defensively.

"Well, excuse me for caring," Lynzi expressed, "but he sure isn't acting like your boyfriend!"

"Caring? Oh no, girlfriend I think you're prying!" I stated in an escalated pitch.

She screamed, "Don't get all crazy on me because your so-called guy is tripping!"

"Huh, you should know about that, as much as Bam has cheated on you!" I yelled back.

"Whatever, Payton!" Lynzi shouted. "If you wanna turn this around, fine. Yeah, I'll be the first to admit that my relationship is rocky. At least I'm acknowledging the fact. I ask you, how can you deal with the situation if you refuse to believe that there is even a problem? I know I wasn't there, but Dymond told me Starr announced she got with Dakari."

"For your information, he practically told me she was lying. So stay out of my business," I blurted out.

Rain came to the car, luckily. You could hear a paper clip drop all the way home. From then on, the conversation was . . . well, there was no conversation. Rain knew something had gone down, but she dared not ask what.

"I don't know, Lord," I said as I knelt on my knees praying before Dakari came. "Maybe I was wrong to get upset with Lynzi. I didn't have to throw in her face how deceitful Bam is, to hurt her like that. Please forgive me. I'll apologize to my dear friend. But she just got under my skin. While we're talking, I must also repent in another area. Only You know that I was annoyed with You earlier today. I just couldn't figure out why You would allow someone else to have my guy. Later, I found out it wasn't true. I'm so sorry for being mad at You. I need Your anointed help daily. Clearly, I see You've got things under control up there! So, I'll back off and let You do Your job. I now know, only You are in charge of controlling my man."

3

Breaking It Off

I had been thinking things over. A lot of things. I love Dakari, and he loves me. In my heart, I know we're meant to be together.

So I started talking to the Lord. "You know, Lord," I whispered, as I continued to pray before my boyfriend came over, "I thank You for hearing my prayers. And even though I know I don't deserve it, You have also answered them. Only You know how strong my feelings are for Dakari. And, well, I almost lost him because I didn't wanna have sex. I can't make that mistake again. I'm ready to be intimate with him, and I plan on going for it tonight. Knowing You like I do, I know this information doesn't sit well. However, God, understand that I love him. For all practical purposes, we're married in my heart. I can't see myself with anyone else. So, before I act on this, I'm asking for forgiveness, even though I kinda, sorta, don't consider this a sin. Hopefully, You won't either, because I can't foresee anything stopping me."

I had been waiting for about an hour. It was now six-thirty in the evening. I started getting paranoid.

"I wonder what could be keeping him," I uttered to myself out loud. "It's not like Dakari to be late. Maybe he doesn't wanna straighten things out after all. Or worse, he could be with Starr."

The thought of the two of them together made my stomach churn. But before I could speculate anymore, my brother stormed through the door. He was huffing and puffing about something.

"What's rattling you?" I asked.

Perry shouted, "Shoot, we just got out of practice. Coach tried to kill us."

"Had Dakari left when you—?" I questioned before being rudely cut off.

"What's up Payton? Why are you asking me about that chump?" my brother asked as he noticed my purse and keys in my hand. "I know you're not waiting for him!"

I stated, "I can handle my relationship, thank you kindly."

"Sis, everyone in the locker room was giving him props for landing the hottest new chick in school. Don't be stupid," my brother said.

Before I could respond, I heard a car horn. So, I grabbed my jacket and dashed out the door. My brother held my arm.

"Be careful!" Perry voiced with concern. "I'm telling you, He is dating that—"

I pulled away saying, "Yeah, yeah, yeah!"

As I walked to the car, I totally ignored Perry's voice. It was like all the things he said went in one ear and out the other. The only thing I could think about was being intimate with my guy.

Gosh, I've dreamed of that moment for years. I wondered,

what would it be like? Would it hurt? Would I be good? Would I satisfy him? Shucks, would I even want to do it again?

I've always imagined it being romantic. You know, candles everywhere; tall ones, fat ones, scented ones, and green ones. Soft music is a must in my dream. Or maybe it should just be spontaneous. In a way, planning it out seems wrong somehow.

"Hey, baby," I began as I entered the car, "where are we going?"

Dakari mumbled, "Over to my crib."

As I leaned over to kiss him on the cheek I replied, "Well, I was thinking about going someplace a little more private."

"My crib will be cool," Dakari explained. "Remember, my folks are in Atlanta with Drake?"

"Oh, yeah, that's right. They're meeting with sports agents. Your place is perfect," I said.

Dakari was unusually quiet. Actually, his silence reminded me of the other day when we drove to Athens. Even though he seemed distant, this time I didn't sweat it. See, I knew that in a few minutes we'd be closer than ever.

"Are you hungry?" Dakari asked when he finally spoke.

I answered, "Yep! How 'bout we go to our favorite place."

"I was just thinking that same thing," Dakari added. "Let's just get it to go though. We really need to spend all of our time talking. What time do you have to be home anyway?"

"Around nine o'clock, since we have school tomorrow," I informed him.

He confidently said, "Oh, you'll be home way before that!"

We pulled into Mr. Tokyo's for Japanese cuisine. This summer we ate here faithfully, once a week. Chicken teriyaki, always the same delicious dish.

As Dakari went in to get the food, I reflected on our summer. We had such a blast. I truly hated it was over. You know the saying, "Opposites attract"? Basically we are the opposite of that statement. Mostly, we like the same things.

Other than being apart for our usual routine of work and practice, we were inseparable. I worked at my dad's dealership, and Dakari worked at J. B. White's Department Store in the men's section. On Fridays we'd both take off and volunteer at the YMCA. We were the best lifeguards they had. All the children loved us.

Much of our fun came when we hung out with the crew. Every weekend it seemed we were into something. But nothing tops the time we went to Savannah.

Lynzi's father is an attorney, and his firm owns a time-share beachfront property. When it was her dad's turn to use the place, he took all of us. Lynzi, Dymond, Rain, and myself stayed in the cabin with her father, Mr. Jackson. He was nice enough to put the guys up in a hotel. We all told Lynzi that her dad was really special to do that. However, she insisted that he only did it out of guilt. She claims he never spends time with her. You see, he lives in Atlanta. He's been there ever since her folks got divorced eight years ago.

Whatever the reason, Mr. Jackson set the place out. We went crabbing, canoeing, hiking, cycling, touring, and best of all, shopping on his dime. The only bad thing was Lynzi's surprise.

Mr. Jackson kept saying, "I've got a surprise for you, baby, and you're going to love it."

Well, we were down there for four days. And the day we were to leave, the surprise came. It, or should I say *she,* was his twenty-eight-year-old fiancée. Needless to say, Lynzi was furious. She pitched such a fit that her dad called off his engagement!

We ate our dinner in the kitchen. As Dakari poured the sodas, I asked him if he remembered our trip to Savannah.

"How could I ever forget," he murmured. "I spent half of my summer earnings on that private dinner cruise. But listen, that's not what I wanna discuss!"

"I've got something to tell you too," I said with a smile.

After we finished gobbling down our food, I grabbed Dakari's hand and led him down the hall. While walking, I was so happy we were together. When we reached his room, I went to kiss him.

"Payton, no," he cautioned. "I really need to tell you something."

"We can talk after," I whispered.

For about three minutes or so, I'd say we were definitely enjoying the passion. Dakari gently caressed his fingers through my head, mangling my flip. Never before had I dared to go any further. But at that moment, I was contemplating everything.

God must not have wanted that for me. For it was at that moment that Dakari pulled away from me. The next words he uttered were shockers.

"I'm not down with this," he informed me while buttoning up his pants.

I retorted, "What do you mean, you don't want this? All you've been talking about was this."

I leaned forward to resume rubbing his chest.

He replied, "Payton, please just sit down and listen to me. This is hard enough on me, without you making it harder. Chill!"

"What!" I said backing off of him and then sitting on the bed. "What's so important that it can't wait 'til after we're intimate?"

"I don't love you!" he dared to say.

"Huh . . . what are you saying? I don't . . . I don't understand," I said softly.

Dakari began, "Remember when we first decided to go together? We made a pact. Don't you know what I'm talking about?"

"Yeah! If one of us ever felt that they didn't want to be committed, then the other . . . " I uttered, not being able to bring myself to say the rest.

"The other would immediately let go with no qualms," he reminded me.

I couldn't believe what I was hearing—Dakari saying he didn't love me. I surely thought I'd never see that day. He went on to say that he wanted out because there was someone else. It didn't take a rocket scientist to know that this other person was the new girl, Starr.

He admitted everything. Last night, he lost his virginity with a complete stranger. I was furious!

"Why would you do this, Dakari? You met this girl last night at the barbecue place. How could you just up and sleep with someone you don't even know? You were suppose to share that moment with me, not some chick you just met!" I shouted while pacing the floor.

He informed, "I've known Starr since the Fourth of July. She wasn't a stranger."

"Are you kidding? You mean you've been cheating on me for two whole months?" I yelled.

"No, Payton," he said calmly. "After you left my house on the Fourth, Drake, his girl, and I headed to the mall. Well, when we got there I let them go their way, so they could have privacy. I just . . . sort of ran into this girl, and we started talking," Dakari stated.

"How could you just sort of run into a girl at the mall and carry on a whole conversation. Something had to attract you to her. For goodness' sake, think about what you're telling me. You'd just left me and we had had a great time over here. If I recall, you came and picked me up later.

39

We went to the base and saw fireworks," I argued.

Dakari responded, "Look, I'm not going there with you. Whether you believe me or not, when Starr and I met, there was nothing between us."

I replied, "Well, if it was so innocent, then when we hooked up that night how come you didn't mention this girl?"

"I didn't even know her myself, really," he remarked. "After that day we talked as friends for weeks. She was new here and she didn't know anybody. So I wanted to help her get—"

Cutting him off, I said with my heart breaking, "If you wanted to help her get adjusted, you could have introduced her to your friends. Nothing more, you should have at least let her meet me. Your GIRLFRIEND!"

"I tried," he demanded, "but she didn't want to meet anyone until school started. That's not even important anymore. The point is, you and I weren't seeing eye-to-eye. I was vulnerable. Starr filled a void that you couldn't."

Tears started to stream down my face like a river as I said, "Yeah, that's what your precious Starr said to me in the hall. Only, I was so stupid that I didn't believe her."

"You gotta believe I didn't mean for you to find out like that," Dakari admitted.

I ran out of the room and locked myself in the bathroom. I was devastated. The pain felt like someone had just stuck a knife in my heart and twisted it. Never before had I felt so alone. This hurt much, much worse than the pain this morning.

All of a sudden I heard something louder than my cry. It was the phone ringing. I settled down to listen to Dakari.

"Hey baby," I heard him say in the sexy voice he always gave to me! "Yeah, I told her, but she's not taking it too well. . . . You can count on it baby. . . . I'll be back soon from dropping her home."

Before he hung up, I heard him make a kissing noise to

the phone. I couldn't take this. There was no way I could allow this newcomer to snatch my man. I went back to his room and started to undress.

"Payton, what? You trippin'," Dakari said, obviously stunned.

I basically attacked him. But throwing myself on him wasn't working. He walked out of the room. I just fell to the floor, with my ego shattered. However, I picked up what little pride I had left and headed to the family room to try a different approach.

"Okay baby, I forgive you. We—we can just put all of this behind us. I know you didn't mean what you said. You love me. This girl, I know she's cute with a nice body and all, but that physical stuff can't compete with what we've built. Don't throw it away. Don't throw us away! I won't let you, Dakari. I can't let you go. Say you won't leave me—say it," I said out of exasperation.

He didn't go for that either. When he rejected me that time, I felt like a huge part of me died. He tried to calm me, but none of his tactics worked.

Dakari pacified me by saying, "You'll get over me in no time. I couldn't let you have sex with me and go against your beliefs. You'll thank me later."

Mom's words came rushing back to me in a flood. "If you have to get a boy that way, he's not worth it. You have to look at the long haul. Is he good for fifty years, or just for a few passionate nights?"

The ride home seemed endless. I wanted to speak, but no words were right. When he dropped me off, I knew that nothing would be the same again.

I could not bring myself to walk in the front door. I knew my brother would be waiting to grill me. Part of me hesitated to admit, even to myself, what had just happened.

Thoughts of Dakari being out of my life were making me lose my mind. I felt that I had to do something. But what?

It quickly became clear that in order to win him back, I had to study the competition. From the earlier phone call, I knew that Dakari would probably be seeing Starr. So, I hopped in my jeep and followed him. I had never before done anything so crazy. However, I'd never been in such dire straits. Starr had what belonged to me, and the only way to get him back was to see what she's got.

Where's he going? I thought to myself as he turned into the shopping center. He went in the grocery store. It was weird that he was in such a rush that he parked haphazardly in the handicapped spot.

"Gosh, he shouldn't be hungry. We just ate. Is he buying food? Oh my, he's gonna cook for her," I said nervously to myself.

About five minutes later, Dakari came bursting out of the store with a bouquet of flowers. They were the prettiest things I'd ever seen when it came to an arrangement. It had all kinds: lilies, tulips, lilacs, and roses. I know it sounds busy; but trust me, they were gorgeous.

"He can't be giving her those!" I uttered in despair.

Shoot, I only got flowers twice. And we dated for two years. Once was for our junior prom and the other time was for my seventeenth birthday this summer. Truthfully, I had to whine and gripe to get those. That's just like a dog. I do all the work, training him and things, only to have some other owner take him and reap the benefits.

When we reached his house, I parked on the street a few houses down. Starr was sitting in her classic red BMW convertible, waiting on him. I was so mad that I was too far away to eavesdrop. When he reached her car door, I thought I was gonna throw up. He gently leaned down and helped her out of the car with his free hand. She stepped out dressed like a floozy, if you asked me, in that faded leopard print minidress.

Even though I thought the dress was ugly, I could tell Dakari loved it. He was twirling her around and all so she could model it. Then from behind his back, he suddenly sprang the flowers. Tacky Starr must have liked his gesture but not necessarily the flowers, the way she tossed them into her car. Then she pulled Dakari close to her, too close for my eyes. When she kissed him, their passion blinded me.

I felt like a real private investigator. The way I was all slumped down in the seat, you'd have thought I had done this before. I don't know why spying came natural, but it did.

Their embrace got so intense that I wondered why they didn't take it inside. How gross! To watch them all over each other in the middle of the street was too much. Granted, it was dark outside, but still! Even though I was against their actions, the thought that Dakari was never that carefree with me made me angrier.

Since they were standing clearly in front of me, I wanted to run them down. Being that this thing had me a tad shaken up, I did something very crazy. I placed my jeep in drive and pressed hard on the gas. The two of them were so preoccupied that they never heard the roaring engine slashing towards them. Somewhere in those sixty feet, I lost my nerve. Slamming on brakes just inches away from them, I stopped.

"ARE YOU CRAZY?" Starr yelled, as my loud horn and bright lights made them unlock from their embrace.

Dakari stepped away from her, saying, "I'll handle this, Starr. Here, take my key and wait for me in the house, please."

As she went inside, she passed by my window and gave me an evil look. Although what I had just done was completely dumb, in a weird way, I felt happy. For a brief moment, I got to break up Dakari and Starr. Boy, was she steaming mad. It was about time that she got to feel some of what I was experiencing. It's like the whole frustrating situation made me feel like a Mack truck had rolled over me.

"So you wanna get out of the car, or what?" Dakari asked.

I exclaimed, "Sure!" as if he had just asked me out on a date.

Before I could shut my door and face him, he shouted, "What's up with this race car stuff? Huh, Payton?"

"Don't yell at me," I demanded.

Dakari said, "I thought I knew you!"

"Yeah," I uttered, "join the club, 'cause I thought I knew you, too!"

"Can't you just accept that it's over between us?" Dakari questioned.

I answered with a most sincere heart, "At this point, I honestly don't know. For the longest time, I've loved you. Goodness, Dakari, you know I wanted to marry you. Now either you were lying all this time or you felt the same way. Which is it?"

"You know I wasn't lying or acting or pretending. None of that. What I felt . . . was deep and real." He paused for a second, then clinched my face with a sensual touch and said, "But Payton, I feel none of those things for you anymore."

Dakari let go of my face just as he finished his last word. He tried to walk away, but I jumped in front of him. I refused to let him just leave me like that. Yet, just before I begged and pleaded, I noticed something different about Dakari that numbed me.

It wasn't his words. It wasn't his actions. It was his eyes. Never had I seen such a stare of frustration. It was finally clear to me that I had lost my guy. Feeling dejected, I said nothing. I just got in my car and left.

44

It was about 10:30 P.M. when I got home. Of course, I got a lecture. My mother must have sensed my despair because she didn't come down that hard on me. She asked me what was wrong, but I couldn't bring myself to open up to her. She'd never understand. Although she liked Dakari, she said on several occasions that I was getting too attached to him. Giving my mom this news might make her night. I couldn't deal with that right now on top of everything else.

My brother didn't ask me, but when I passed his room I told him it was over with Dakari. Growing up, Perry always loved to prove me wrong. However, I guess he knew I was already wounded too badly to sustain another blow. He didn't hurt me worse by saying, "I told you so!"

Both Perry and I had had our own separate phone lines for a few years now. As I washed my face in the bathroom that was adjoining to both our rooms, I heard his line ring. It was clear that he was talking about me.

"Yep, she's back," he said softly in the receiver, hoping I could not hear. "I don't know what that chump said. . . . She didn't go into details. . . . Yeah, you should dial her up. I know she needs to commiserate with someone. . . . Oh, I don't care. You can tell her I told you . . . She should know it was out of luv. . . . Peace, Rain, bye!"

I was so out of it. About fifteen minutes later, my phone rang. How quickly I had forgotten that it was probably Rain.

I answered the phone with hope saying, "Dakari?"

"You gotta let it go, Payton," I heard Dymond's voice say through the phone. "It's not Dakari. It's us."

"Hello!" Rain said.

"Hey," Lynzi uttered.

I asked them, "Who called who?" sounding agitated, but clearly deep down I was glad to hear from them.

"I called Dymond. Dymond called Lynzi, on the three-way. Then Miss Lynzi called you," Rain explained.

"Getting to the point," Dymond said frankly, "we just called to let you know, we know! You know, about you and Dakari breaking up. Not to be insensitive, but you must get over that jerk."

Lynzi started with caution in her tone, "I know we had it out earlier, but you know I love ya. You're my girl. Dymond's right for a change. Don't let this keep you down."

"We're here for you, Payton. Whatever you do, don't close yourself off from us," piped up Rain.

I uttered, "I don't know what you guys expect from me. I have no supernatural strength. All I know is that it feels like my main organ has been donated without my permission. Someone has given my heart to Starr Love and I'm left to die. Believe me, I'm trying with everything in me to hold it together. But, guys . . . this hurts. I wanna be strong. It's just not that easy . . . it's not easy breaking it off!"

4

Crying
with Brian

*T*he next few weeks were extremely tough for me. From dealing with people asking me why we broke up, to seeing Dakari and his new 'Love' everywhere, I had no peace. Life without the guy of my heart was as hard as I expected. Every place I went, everything I ate, everyone I knew, every outfit I wore, and every Brian McKnight song I heard reminded me, in some way or another, of my terrible loss.

I was angry. Angry at not only Dakari Ross Graham, but angry at the world. When I really searched deep down inside myself, I discovered who I truly blamed. After weeks of not being able to pray, nor wanting to listen to my many gospel CDs, I realized that I was angry with God.

God had never forsaken me like this. My life up until now was rosy! I had wonderful parents, who were both influential and well-off. All four of my grandparents were still alive. A crazy younger brother who, although annoying at times, I wouldn't trade for a dollar. Maybe ten dollars.

Naw, I'm just kidding. The best of friends. A beautiful house to live in. Smarts! And on top of all that, God even threw in a pretty cool personality. I mean, He's always given me every desire of my heart. So now, why all of a sudden would He change stuff for me?

Brian McKnight is my favorite R & B artist. There's not a Friday night that I don't unwind to his sultry sound. His voice, oh, it's heavenly! If he wasn't married and I was years older, I wouldn't be sweatin' this Dakari thang. Shoot, I'd be headed to Hollywood to meet the man whose tenor voice gives me chills.

For years, there was only one of Brian's songs that I had a problem with. It's titled, "Oh Lord," cut number twelve on his first album. For the longest, I couldn't figure out how my favorite artist could sing about someone being so bitter with God. Well, I guess at that time I hadn't experienced my own disappointment.

That song clung to my soul one day at school. Three weeks had gone by, but my pain was still fresh. It was lunch-time and I was sitting two tables down from the whole crew. Dakari and Starr were a part of this bunch. My girlfriends wanted me to eat with them. They claimed that they didn't understand why I could not join the group. I told them that I couldn't figure out why they'd think I would want to.

So, I ate alone. During my sorrow, I pulled out my head-phones and played my Brian McKnight CD. I was in such a daze that I did not focus on most of the album. However, I did comprehend "Oh Lord." The moment I heard those words and that music, something in me clicked. I may as well have stood on the table with a mike in hand and sung the song myself. That was just how much I felt the song.

Instead of singing the words I could never relate to before, I sat very quietly, reflecting on why I felt the same way. It was like that musical piece was written just for me. Never had I felt so far removed from God.

As I turned my head toward our cafeteria's well-lit ceiling, I talked with God in silence. I thought, "You know, Lord, this song Brian is singing truly expresses my own thoughts. I mean, I wonder, do You even hear me up there. I've been down here prayin' for weeks. Things are extremely tough and I don't know if I've got the strength to keep facing this. Sometimes I really wonder why You made me. If You won't pick me up when I'm down, then who will?"

I paused and looked toward the group. Continuing in my thoughts, "Shoot, does anyone really care? Let me know something, Lord. Are Your ears open? Am I praying hard and long enough? I can't find my way. Why is that? Are the doors of heaven closed to me? Is it my destiny to be alone for the rest of my life, never finding ever again what I had and felt for Dakari? I can't even hang out with my girls. They don't understand me. Does what I want even matter? I'm waiting on You to answer some of these questions. In Your Word it says to trust in You. So, I'm really trying to hang in here. However, my world is getting crazier by the day. Please, rescue me. Please Lord!"

The bell that ended lunch also ended my prayer. Even though I had shared with God, I didn't feel calm. Truthfully, I had no idea whether or not God was gonna respond to my plea. However, I did believe that if He intervened, things would miraculously be alright.

As the day went on, my depression got worse. I couldn't eat any of my dinner. Feelings of sickness came all over me. My knees began to buckle and my nose started to twitch.

That night was far and beyond the worse I've ever had. I had suicidal thoughts. I was so down that I didn't see any purpose in continuing to live with such pain. Since my problems wouldn't go away, ending my life seemed to be the only way out.

My mother told me that I seemed stressed out. She suggested that I use their bathroom and relax in the jacuzzi. That was a great idea. I grabbed my one-liter bottle of purified water and my cassette box with Brian McKnight's CD.

The hot water felt so good. Before I got in, I turned off all the lights, except the one in my mom's closet. The darkness, solitude, and soaking made my worn-out body feel good. However, as I listened to the song "After the Love," basically I still felt awful.

"Why does each line of this dumb song sing my story? Dang it Brian, I used to listen to your music and get romantically inspired. Now, I'm just an emotional basketcase," I uttered out of despair.

Even though the song was making me sad, it actually helped me grasp how I was really feeling. Brian's music tapped into my soul. His songs became a part of me. In some ways, he was my only friend, the only one who could relate to my situation. With the warm washcloth over my face, and suds covering my relaxed body, I swayed, rocked, moved, and danced all underwater to the beat.

"Yep, I'm yearning for ya, Dakari! Why is it over? You belong with me . . . hugging me . . . kissing me! Why is it so hard to accept this? I sure would have held on to my heart, 'cause letting you have it did nothing for me!" I shouted.

We planned our life together. Three kids; boy, girl, boy. A four-thousand-square-foot house in Atlanta. Two BMWs and a Lexus Jeep. After he was done in the NFL, he was gonna be a sports agent. I was planning to be a TV anchor woman, maybe a sportscaster on ESPN or something. We wanted stocks, bonds, 401K, mutual funds, and other savings. Hopefully, we would have been financially set. How could I let this awesome dream go?

I sang out of key, "How can I go on and on and on?"

Saying that made me again think of what ending my life would be like. Surely no one would miss me. They might weep for a few days, but they'd be over it quickly. I mean, how important am I really?

How can I do it though? I pondered as I hit the Jacuzzi button. *I don't own a gun . . . even though I'd never splatter my brains. Uh uh, I ain't going out like that. Pills? Yeah, I could overdose. Nope, I should just get in my car and run off the road. Naw, after I'm gone my dad's insurance would double, and I've already made it go up enough. Hey, I could just slide under this water and not come up. Then it would be over, done, and I'd be gone.*

Even though my world was crazy and it seemed like things weren't getting better, something in me knew I couldn't ever take my own life. You see, without saying another word, I didn't go under. I got out! Out of the tub and out of my pity.

Homecoming was early for us this year. I didn't know who nominated me for queen, but I was one of three finalists. Actually, as surprised as I was to learn that I had made the court, I was even more bewildered to learn that Starr Love had made it too. How ridiculous! People here didn't even know her.

The week had been pretty fun for me. Things seemed to be turning around. My good ole spunky spirit was back. With that attitude, I reunited with my friends.

I must say, I really missed hanging out with the girls. Lately, Lynzi and Rain hadn't ridden to school with me. I made up some story about having to go up to the dealership in the mornings. But I think they knew that I didn't wanna be bothered.

That Monday after school the four of us went to the Howard James restaurant. I apologized for being such a jerk. Reluctantly, they admitted that they could have been more understanding.

"It still hurts," I told them, "but I plan to get through

this. Dakari has moved on. So, I will too! Somehow . . . some way."

The week flew by. Friday was such a busy day. The football team and cheerleaders had a big breakfast in the cafeteria that morning. First through third periods, I was out of classes because of SGA. We had to finalize parade plans.

Lunch was crazy. The school was so hyped up. Dr. Franklin even let up a bit. He allowed us to play rap music during lunch. Dymond, of course, took the privilege as far as she could. She and Fatz were dancing to every hit. After about three songs, others joined in.

I didn't have to go to fourth, fifth, or sixth periods either. The latter part of the day was pep rally time. The routine we did was so sharp! Not braggin', but Lynzi and I made it up.

When they announced the Homecoming Court, I got the loudest cheers. I was pleasantly surprised. Secretly, I hoped that the big applause meant lots of votes.

The parade was the best it had ever been. Everyone thought it was a huge success. Since I was SGA vice president, the parade was mostly my responsibility. Therefore, I begged and pleaded until my dad let the school borrow twenty cars for the occasion. I did work it out so that he got free media coverage. I think he sold two hundred cars for the month of October. The average was one hundred fifty, both new and pre-owned. Most of the folks that bought said they were impressed with my dad's commitment to serving the community through education.

My mother was so excited that I made the court. She loved that kind of stuff. She bought me the cutest suit to strut in that night. It was gray and red, our school colors.

When halftime came, I was so nervous. Luckily, our cheerleading sponsor let me leave the field during the second quarter to change out of my uniform. At the half, we were up by twenty-one points. Already Dakari had one hundred and one rushing yards and three touchdowns. Before we were announced onto the field, Starr was quick to point that out.

"Did you see MY man get off out there?" she asked as she rudely bumped into me.

I didn't degrade myself by giving her an answer. Also, I hated to admit that I still watched every move number twenty made. As I looked over, I noticed my dad making small talk with Mr. Love. Starr's father was the new judge in town. Even though I was disgusted, I couldn't be too mad. My dad was just being himself. He always makes it a point to know all the movers and shakers personally. He calls it "smart business." I call it brown nosing. Though I would not dare tell him that.

Soon it was time to take the field. It was hard to keep calm. My dad eased my tension when he whispered the nicest words as he escorted me.

"Regardless of the outcome, Payton, your mother and I are truly proud of you. You're an excellent student. You are in all kinds of good stuff. Your peers think enough of you to vote you this far. And my princess, . . . you're so beautiful. In my book, you've already blossomed into a queen," he softly spoke.

Finally, the long walk on the cold, ruffled-up turf ended. All eyes were on us, the five candidates. The next words I remember hearing were those of Dr. Franklin over the intercom.

"And this year's Homecoming Queen—like it's a surprise to anyone—is none other than Miss Payton Autumn Skky!" Dr. Franklin voiced with excitement. "Congratulations!"

I was so happy. Being Queen was a great feeling, but beating Starr was justice. We weren't even, but I was getting close.

At the dance afterwards, I was the center of attention. So many guys wanted to dance with the gal that wore the crown. Things were going great. Even though I didn't have a date, I didn't feel out of place.

After dancing on six straight fast songs, I finally sat down. As I drank the punch, I realized that I was glad to be seated. You see, that's when the slow songs started to play. The last thing I wanted was a yucky guy breathin' all over me.

I was having a great time. The thought of Starr and Dakari being together hadn't entered my mind. However, when I saw them hugged up on the dance floor, my smile immediately turned to a frown. This whole week I had convinced myself that I could deal with this. Unfortunately, that dream was shattered when I saw the guy I still loved embracing another.

Ironically, the disc jockey was playing Brian McKnight's song "One Last Cry!" Like the other day, every word he sang was my truth. I had a broken heart and I was alone. A tear rolled down my cheek as I thought about giving him my all. Worse, my all wasn't enough to keep him.

Just as I tried to hold back the tears, I was saddened even more. I witnessed Dakari kiss her. It was slow, long, sultry, and sloppy. I sprang to my feet and dashed out the door.

Rain stopped me before I left and said, "Why are you upset? You won!"

"Yeah, I've got the stupid crown," I said pitifully, "but Starr's got the guy. I tell ya, Rain, she's got the better prize."

That weekend, I slipped back into a depressed state. No visitors. No phone. No fun. Just thoughts of Dakari and songs from Brian.

When Saturday morning hit, I couldn't bring myself to get up out of bed. My dad was at work. My mom was at her sorority meeting. Perry was somewhere in the streets with his friends. Therefore, no one bothered me. I just lay there.

"Dang," I mumbled, "I let the CD play all night."

I remember so clearly when Dakari gave me Brain McKnight's second album. It was Valentine's Day, and he took me to the Olive Garden restaurant. After our delicious meal, we came back to my house and exchanged gifts. My parents were really good about giving us some privacy. They trusted us up in the bonus room. Well, only after my dad had a man-to-man talk with Dakari. He never told me what exactly my father said. I do know that based on Dakari's actions, or should I say, "lack thereof," that my dad had earned his respect.

Our February fourteenth was simple, yet special. We toasted to chilled sparkling apple cider and he presented me with a bouquet of red roses. Dancing to my gift with three lit candles made the evening unforgettable. I still remember part of our conversation as if it were yesterday.

"You hear this song?" Dakari asked.

I replied, "Yeah, number six."

"Well, it's called "Still in Love," Dakari stated. "I'm not as crazy about this dude as you are, but I must give him props for the cut. It's the bomb."

"Violets turn red . . . and roses . . . blue? What?" I questioned. "You're right, I love Brian's material, but this tune isn't making sense."

He responded, "No, no, you've gotta listen closely. Basically, the words are saying when things in life are crazy, or totally out of the norm, he'll still be in love."

"Oh, OK, I hear it now," I said, still slow dancing in his arms. "Wow, that's so sweet."

Dakari spoke with passion, "And that's how I feel for you."

"What do you mean?" I questioned, basically knowing the answer, but just wanting to hear him explain and make me feel all oozy inside.

"Let's just say, when cheerleaders wear football pads and jocks wear skirts, I'll still be in love!" he said with a smile.

Hearing that tune in the background made thinking about that precious moment unbearable. I wept in my bed. I sobbed so hard and long that I gave myself a headache. My pillow was dripping wet. My sheet was drenched. My spread was soaked. Even my flannels were damp!

"I thought you'd be in love with me forever! I guess all I've got left of you is tears," I mumbled.

Finally, at three o'clock in the afternoon, I got up. After nearly a day of crying incessantly, I tried to pull it together and go on with life.

My mother made keeping busy easy, since she left a long list of chores to complete. My afternoon was filled with washing dishes, folding clothes, and mopping the floor. And as if that weren't enough, I had to go to the dreaded grocery store.

Piggly Wiggly is always crowded on the weekends. The whole time I was there, I moped about why my mom sent me. One would've thought I was buying for the entire neighborhood, with all that stuff on her list.

Another thing that gets me is that some items must be a specific name brand. I mean, like she'd have rice, but I couldn't get any rice. It had to be Lipton. The same thing with paper towels. Bounty was the only kind she wanted. Being that her list was not only long, but particular as well, finding everything took forever.

I was almost done when I thought I was hearing things. I was placing Kraft cheese in the buggy, when I just knew I heard Brain McKnight's voice. After I shook my head, as if to shake the sound away, the music would not stop. I then realized that I wasn't crazy. The store was playing "Crazy Love" over the speaker. Michael Bolton's rendition of "Georgia" had just finished playing.

"Yep, that's Brian singing all right. Like I really need to

hear this now," I uttered as I strolled down the aisle.

While reaching for the Pillsbury cinnamon rolls, I wondered how this song related to my lost love. I knew that I was still head over heels for Dakari. When we were dating, I felt like I was at home every time I was around him. He was so adventurous. He definitely kept me on edge, and gave me crazy love.

On my bad days, he'd always find a way to make them bright. I depended on his strength. Maybe that's why I'm so miserable now. For you see, if it had not been him that hurt me, I'd be headed straight to him for healing. I was closer to Dakari than I was to Rain. She and I were tight. We've been best buddies ever since we were three. Preschool, Brownies, elementary, ballet, jazz, Girl Scouts, gymnastics, middle school, piano, Cadets, junior high, you name it, Rain and I did it together. Yet, all that closeness switched to Dakari the day he and I made our commitment official.

After an hour and a half, I was at the cash register. I checked my mom's list twice. Probably, some way, somehow, I still would manage to forget something.

"Gosh, this is a lot of grub!" my friend Duke exclaimed as he bagged my groceries. "Ya'll havin' a jam, Miss Home Town Royalty?"

I answered, "See, now why you trippin'? You just started working here this week. Believe it or not, this is our regular amount."

"Yeah, I forgot yo' pops got bank," Duke blurted out.

"Are you happy?" I asked.

Duke nodded his head and said, "Oh ya, I'm straight!"

"Well, be glad! All the money in the world can't buy happiness," I said.

He watched me leave, puzzled at my statement. I didn't care.

57

It was early Saturday evening, and finally I was relaxing, watching "Good Times." Dakari was nowhere in my brain. The couch felt so good. Then in walked my brother. By the way he was smirking, I knew he wanted something.

"Sis, I need a favor. Please drive me and Tori to the show. Mom said she'd scoop us up. I'll owe ya one," Perry begged.

Dang! I didn't want to get up, but I really liked Tori. I truly thought she was a good match for Perry. She was a year younger than him. Since he couldn't see her at school, being that ninth graders go to junior high, I didn't mind helping a brother out.

When I started up the car, the song "Goodbye" came on in the middle of the cut. I was listening to it earlier. I just couldn't seem to shake Brian and the slow tunes.

"What's up with this mess?" Perry demanded.

I yelled, "Wait a minute! Don't raise your voice at me. Shucks, you ain't even old enough to drive. Yet, here you are trying to act all grown."

"Hey, I ain't mean to yell or nothin', but this song is depressin.' Listen at this. What's he sayin'? I hope you stay . . . I watch you leave . . . I'm crazy 'cause you won't come back . . . I blame myself . . . ," Perry voiced before I cut him off.

"OK, OK," I said.

"No wonder you've been locked in your room all sad. It's this!" said Perry.

I didn't respond. Probably because I knew my baby brother was right. There was no way I could admit it though. So, I just drove.

Perry broke the silence by saying, "Isn't there a gospel tune on this CD?"

"Yeah right, like I wanna hear anything about God," I murmured. "The Lord has forgotten me, or should I say He literally took away my most important organ, my heart!"

"Oh, you're trippin' sis. It says in Job chapter 22 that the

58

Lord giveth and the Lord taketh away. But through it all, blessed be the name of the Lord. God ain't put ya down. He's probably lookin' out for ya. Plus, if Dakari's eyes can be that easily swayed, then you ain't need him no way," my brother voiced, sounding almost like a Bible scholar.

All day Sunday, I pondered on what my brother said. Perry was so right. How could I be so fickle with God? I recalled that His Word says that even when we're in the melting pot, He's there. He's waiting to refine us, before He pulls us out.

At church, I really didn't pay too much attention to the service, unfortunately. All through it, I felt so unworthy. I prayed in silence the entire time.

I said in my mind, "Lord, I haven't chatted with You in a while, but it's me, Payton Skky. I know I've been a fair-weather Christian: with You when You give me what I want, and forgetting about You when I'm disappointed. Please forgive me. I now realize that You love me, far more than I could ever love Dakari. That's been my problem. I've been so focused on what You haven't done for me that I never once looked at what's important. And that is doing what I need to do to stay close to You, not him. Lord, I was willing to displease You in order to please Dakari. Talk about backwards. I'm so sorry! Thanks for intervening."

I had never fully listened to the cut "Coming Back Again." That day, however, I must have played Brian's gospel tune twenty times or more. Hearing about Jesus' ultimate sacrifice put things into perspective. I learned that if God never did another thing for me, having His only Son die for my sins was alone worth me praising Him forever.

For if God seemed further away from me through all this, I had to ask myself a question. Who moved? To handle this pain the way I did, it was obvious that I strayed. God was always there.

"OK," I said to myself as I packed my two Brian McKnight compact discs away, "no more moping, no more feeling sorry for myself, and no more crying with Brian!"

5

Meeting the Debs

"Payton, I'm leaving," my mother said as she peeked into my room. "Now are you driving, dear?"

"No ma'am! Me, Lynzi, and Rain are riding with Dymond," I replied, while I flat ironed my hair.

My mother shouted out, "Lynzi, Rain, and I . . . Payton, you know better. Please do not attend this meeting talking any ole way. Remember honey, you are a debutante. That is, a young lady who is refined and well educated. Not some back-alley, verb-splitting girl."

I laughed under my breath and uttered, "OK, Mother dear, I will not embarrass you."

After making that statement, I scooted past my mother who was standing in my doorway. Yes, I had such an attitude. Grinding my teeth and shaking my head as I walked to the bathroom, my mother knew I was angry. I mean, how dare she think that I didn't know how to carry myself. This was the main reason why I had reservations about being in the cotillion. I knew my mom would expect me to be "the perfect deb."

"Look Payton, I'm sorry if I offended you, sweetheart," my mother said hesitantly. "I just want you to get something meaningful out of this whole experience. I realize that you have been around this event for some time. Helping me with the girls every year has been great for me. Even though you may feel negative about participating, give it a chance. I promise you, if you enter into this with an open mind, what you will receive from the experience is going to surpass anything you can imagine."

After those brief words, my mom left, but not until she made sure she told me to be on time. Dymond has a tendency to run on "CP" time. So I'd already decided that if she wasn't here in twenty minutes, I would drive myself. I didn't want to hear my mom's mouth if I showed up after things started, and being late was a pet peeve of mine as well.

Even though I have watched the Links groom girls, I didn't know how I'd feel getting groomed. A lot of the stuff we will learn, I already know. I was raised with a charm-school mentality. Sometimes, I don't know whether that's good or bad!

As I waited by the door for my friends to arrive, several questions came to mind. For starters, will this be fun? Will my mother attend every function? Will it be messy being around all those girls? Who will be my escort? I pondered on that question until my ride came. After all, I didn't have a boyfriend.

———————

"Maybe I should just face facts, suck it up, and tell my mom I'm quitting," I uttered aloud to my friends as Dymond drove sixty-five miles per hour in a residential zone, trying to hurry us there.

Dymond yelled, "Yeah right, Payton! Your mom would have a heart attack. She's been livin' for the year 'her baby' would be in the ball. What is this, her eighth or ninth year being involved?"

"Nope," I answered just knowing crazy Dymond was right about my mother being terribly disappointed. "This is her eleventh year working with the debs."

"Girl, you'll find a date," Rain stated with a positive voice.

I replied in a hesitant tone, "I don't know. Shoot—for me, there's not even a prospect."

"Well, you're not the only one that's having date problems," Lynzi voiced.

"What Bam done NOW?" Dymond asked.

Lynzi answered quickly, "Basically, I caught his butt in some lies!"

"WHHHAT? Naw girl! Keep talking and get to the juicy stuff," Dymond interjected.

"Dy," I said as I popped her on the head, "ya know that's messed up!"

"Ouch, that hurt Payton!" Dymond replied. "I'm just sayin' what you and Rain are thinkin'. What's up with her and Bam?"

"Like I said, before being rudely interrupted, he got caught lying. I don't have proof, but I think he's messing around on me again. Listen to this, ya'll. Last night after the game, I wanted him to come over to my house. Mind you, I was all alone and he knew this! My mom was with her boyfriend. Bam turned me down. Said he had to hang out with the fellas at Howard's," Lynzi said, obviously getting frustrated.

Dymond cut in and said, "But you and I was at Howard's last night."

"Yeah," Lynzi stated, "that's my point. Did you see Bam anywhere?"

"No, buuut . . . you never told me to look for him or that he was supposed to be there."

"Yeah, that's 'cause I was embarrassed," Lynzi blurted

63

out. "When I talked to him this morning, I never mentioned that I was at Howard's, and do you know that chump went on and on about how much fun he had there all night."

"Men," I uttered.

Dymond said, "You mean boys."

"I know that's right!" Lynzi laughed.

I must say, the Links do everything in style. This first meeting was not only orientation but also a formal luncheon. The function was held at the Hilton Plaza Hotel. The room was so nice, most folks in town have their wedding receptions there. And the tables were beautifully decorated.

I remember Dymond saying, "Dag ya'll, I've never seen a spread this laid out. Ya'll know in the projects, we don't go through all this. We're just glad to eat, period. Ya know what I'm sayin.'"

It was so upscale. Not only were there tons of silverware: appetizer forks, salad forks, dinner forks, and dessert forks, but each place setting had a name tag. Now, I've been to several formal dinners, but never was my name at my seat. Even though it was cute, it was not cool. Shoot, the four of us were at different tables. We probably would have switched them had there not been a seating chart boldly posted at the front entrance.

The tables seated six. Five debutantes and one Links member. My mother had to sit at the head table, since she was the chapter vice president. I was so glad she couldn't eat with me, 'cause I knew if she did, my every movement would be criticized.

Mrs. Ann Smith, my godmother, was my table hostess. After finding that out, I thought my mom might as well have been sitting there herself. See, she and Mrs. Smith are best friends. The two of them are tighter than tight. If I'd had a camcorder, I would have turned it on. This most definitely would save Mrs. Smith from having to recall my every move, only to repeat it later to my mom.

Despite the fact that she blabs a lot, Auntie Ann and I are cool. She and her husband are the best godparents a girl could want. Seems like I get gifts for everything. When I made cheerleading, she gave me a Fashion Fair makeup kit.

"You need to make certain that you look adorable at all times. Cheerleaders are supposed to be cute. Remember that," Auntie Ann said.

Also, every time I made the straight-A honor roll, she'd give me twenty dollars per A. Sometimes that motivated me more than the GPA. Her gifts have now switched from balloons and toys to clothes and jewelry. I'll never forget what she gave me when she found out that I had a steady boyfriend. She took me to lunch and pulled out a diary.

"Now that you've got some business," she leaned over and explained, "you'll need this. Live life, then write in your diary. But Payton, dear, manage to keep it far away from your mother."

There were five debutantes, including myself, whose mothers were Links. How come all five of us were assigned to the same table? Our table number one was positioned directly front and center. It doesn't take Einstein to tell you that this wasn't a coincidence. Our mothers, probably mine in particular, planned this.

In Augusta there are three high schools that are always in competition. My school, Laney, is undoubtedly better than Glenn Hills and T. W. Josey. Actually, speaking frankly, they all have some kinda problem or another. Unfortunately, what majority black high school doesn't nowadays? But tradition has taught us that whichever of the three schools you happen to attend, that's the best!

When I arrived at our table, the only empty seat was mine. Of course when I glanced at my mother up front, she shook her head with displeasure. Besides knowing Mrs.

Smith, I also knew Summer Wright. Her mom is president of the chapter.

Summer and I are kinda cool. We attend the same church. But this girl is very siddity. The only reason she respects me is because my daddy's net worth is more than hers. However, her father does very well. He is the CEO of the largest bank in the area. Sadly, no one in our church youth group cares too much for her. Actually, she gets on my nerves most of the time as well. I've just learned to tolerate her.

See, Summer's main problem is that she brags too much. This Halle Berry look-alike is extremely beautiful and talented—so talented that her parents sent her to the Davidson School of Fine Arts.

"Well hello, Miss Skky," Summer voiced in a condescending tone, as I pulled my chair back.

"Hey, Summer," I said turning toward Auntie Ann, hoping Summer wouldn't continue the conversation.

However, she didn't get the hint 'cause immediately she said, "We've sure got the best seats in the house . . . as well as the best company."

I guess she figured being at the table with rich girls made her stock go up. I, on the other hand, thought the company would make for a boring afternoon. That thought was confirmed when Summer continued to irk me with her every annoying word.

"Payton, do you know everyone?" Summer asked.

I stated boldly, "No!"

"Then let me introduce you," she insisted. "First of all, darling, we've all got something in common. Our mothers are all Links. This, to my immediate left, is Erin Williams. She attends Glenn Hills. Her father owns all the Church's Chickens in the area. And these are the twins, Morgan and Madison Jones. They cheer at T. W. Josey. Their dad is a radiologist, right?"

"Yep," Madison answered.

"Nice to meet you all," I said. "If I'm not mistaken, I think we beat Glenn Hills and T. W. Josey this season."

Erin chuckled and said, "Laney just got lucky this year. We'll get you in basketball."

"Yeah, OK," I muttered.

Summer said, "I hear congrats are in order, Miss Homecoming Queen. I do not see how you did it. Getting all those votes, I mean. From what I'm told, you had some stiff competition."

"I'm just real," I honestly stated.

The four of them talked through lunch, or should I say gossiped through lunch. I simply kept my responses to a minimum. Basically, I only enjoyed Mrs. Smith.

During dessert, which was a delicious chocolate mousse, I was touched on the back. When I looked over my shoulder, it was Dymond giving me a signal to head to the ladies' room. As I excused myself from the table, Summer grabbed my arm.

"How did she become a debutante? Doesn't she live in . . . you know, the projects?" Summer rudely asked with her nose in the air staring down at my friend.

I wanted to go off. No, actually I wanted to hit her. Luckily, Auntie Ann overheard the spoiled witch. She stepped in and rescued me, before I did or said something I'd regret.

"Summer dear, what's your grade point average?" my godmother politely asked, yet giving me a look like she had some ulterior purpose to the question!

"I've got a 3.0," Summer smiled and said with pride.

Auntie Ann looked directly in her eye and said, "Well, being that I was on the selection committee, I just happen to remember that the young lady you were just inquiring about has a 4.0. Now, if she knew your GPA was that much lower than hers, she might be inclined to ask how you got accepted."

Walking to the restroom, I thought about how awesome my godmother is. I was so impressed with the way she approached the whole stinky situation. Auntie Ann had such poise, yet she was effective in getting Summer straight. When I left the table, Summer's face was cracked and on the ground.

Mind you now, neither of the four of us actually had to use the bathroom. When we went together, it was more of a lipstick exchange: putting on fresh lipstick and exchanging information.

"Guess who's sitting at my table?" Rain murmured in a soft voice, yet knowing we all had no clue.

Dymond voiced with frustration, "Girl, why you always trying to make somebody guess. We don't know who in the—"

"Dy, do not even go there," I interrupted, catching her before the language got foul.

Rain then moved from beside Lynzi and crossed the room till she stood by me. Even though she insisted on playing this dumb guessing game, her look of intensity was uncanny. When she made this statement I could have fainted.

"Who would be the last person you'd want to be in this cotillion, Payton? Uh-huh, that's right . . . Her! Starr Love is sitting with me," Rain said in disgust.

I just stood there. Frozen in time. It felt like my heart stopped beating. Part of me hoped Rain was joking. Deep down though, I knew my best friend could never play such a cruel joke.

Lynzi broke the silence. "No way. Her name was not on the list they sent with the acceptance letter."

"You know I had a bad feeling earlier about being in this thing. Now, I know I'm gonna quit!" I yelled.

Dymond stated with authority, "Yeah, right! I don't think so. You can't let the girl get the best of you."

"That's easy for you to say, Dy!" I declared. "It was bad enough that I had to deal with the fact that Dakari isn't gonna escort me. But I'll be doggoned if I stand around and watch him be someone else's date. That's just crazy. All the rehearsals . . . seeing them together. I can't—I know I can't."

Before the tear that was very close to revealing my deep sadness fell, the bathroom door opened. In walked Summer and Starr. They were deep in conversation. They stopped blabbing when they saw us.

"Miss Skky, you know my cousin, Starr," Summer voiced while smiling.

Lynzi imposed and asked, "Your cousin?"

"Oh yes. Her father the Honorable Judge Love is my mother's brother," Summer bragged with pride. "It's funny. When mother first asked Starr to be a debutante, she declined. But when she found out the details, like who was in it . . . that we'd have escorts . . . and lots of close dancing, well my dear cousin quickly changed her mind."

Dymond said under her breath, "Huh, I just bet she did change her mind."

"I bet you just wanted to show off that new boyfriend of yours, right Cuz?" Summer questioned.

Starr just laughed. Smoke was coming from all my girl-friends' ears. I was so devastated. All I could do was cut between them and exit the ladies' room. At least I knew what strings were pulled to get Miss Starr into the cotillion. The thought of this world being filled with people getting ahead based solely on who they know made me sick. Starr didn't even have to interview. Surely she would not have made it. I mean,who would she possibly win over with her disgusting personality?

As I walked back to my seat, I truly felt I could have crawled under a rock and stayed there 'til spring. That way, this whole mess would be over. My mother was talking to Auntie Ann, when I got back to my chair. Unfortunately, seeing her excitement over me in this stupid deb thing convinced me that I had to stick it out.

After our wonderful meal, which consisted of Cornish hens over rice pilaf, with a side of mixed vegetables and assorted rolls, we met in the meeting room next door. Luckily, there were no assigned seats. This meant I sat beside my friends. By this point, I was about tired of Summer and Starr. They were purposely sitting behind me, snickering away.

All of the debs had to stand and introduce themselves and say where they planned to attend college. The other question we all had to answer was, "Why are you proud to be chosen as a debutante?" I've never heard so many versions of the same answer. Basically, everyone said, "Being a deb will help prepare me to be a productive woman of society," in one way or another.

Obviously, our responses were pleasing to the Links because they were all smiles. And when Tori's mom, the president, addressed the group, she made mention of it. Then Mrs. Wright gave us an overview of what to expect from this year.

She began, "Well, young ladies, first of all, on behalf of the Augusta chapter of the Links, Incorporated, I must say we all feel like you all are our finest selections ever. This is just the first of many meetings we'll have together before we present you to society, on April first in our Twenty-First Annual Debutante Cotillion. If you'll pull out your personalized planners that we've given to you, you can follow along as I go over this season's agenda."

While Mrs. Wright talked on, I decided to have a one-on-one with God. I didn't mean to tune her out. My heart just needed to tell my heavenly Father a few important things.

"You know, Lord," I uttered to myself, "I don't thank You enough for the roots that You bore me into this world with. I mean, my dad makes six figures and my mom is a social butterfly. Basically, I have no material need. I know that only You have allowed my family to prosper the way that we have. Even though I'd much rather be here with this bunch of ritzy girls than constantly hoping and dreaming about this type of lifestyle from the projects, being where I am does have its problems. Why is there so much competition? Why are most of these girls fake? Everyone is trying to be the best. Wanting to have on the cutest clothes. Must have the flyy-est hairstyle. And worst of all, I'm just as guilty as they are! You see, I'm the only girl here who is Homecoming Queen for her school. Lord, that makes me feel too good. Not because it's a great honor, but mostly I'm proud because I've accomplished something that none of them could do. However, all of them wished they did. How shallow of me! I know You know this about me already, but by confessing it to You, I feel challenged to change. Help me change, dear Lord. Help me not place myself on a pedestal. That spot belongs to You. Well, thanks for listening."

Coming out of my prayer, I overheard Summer and Starr chattering behind me. I was trying hard not to listen, only when they mentioned Dakari, my ears perked up like Dumbo.

"Dakari said you guys had a great time last night," Starr said to Summer, pumping her ego up.

Summer replied, "We had a blast! Thanks for hooking us up. He's one of those bad boys. You know, the ones your mother tells you to watch out for, nevertheless, the attraction is too strong to resist. We're like magnets. Opposites . . . "

"Attract. Yeah, I know. I've had more than my share of those," Starr responded.

Deep down I also felt that Summer was not the Goody

Two-shoes she claimed to be. So, I wonder who the guy was that they were referring to. I knew one thing for sure. If Summer was interested, he had to come from money. She might take bad boy over good boy, but she'd never date poor boy over rich boy.

"Bam and I—" Summer said to her cousin.

I couldn't even hear the rest. Bam? What? So, that's where his two-timing butt was last night. Although angry and confused, I forced myself to listen.

"Cuz, you said he was rough and tough. Well, I did not find that to be true at all. He was an absolute gentleman. Ooh, he took me to that expensive restaurant down on Broad Street. We had a blast. He did manage to get a little fresh towards the end," Summer admitted.

Starr blurted out, "You shoulda gave it up!"

"Shhh!" Summer stated firmly. "Oh no, not on the first date."

"Don't be no fool. That's how that girl lost my man," Starr said boldly.

I just knew she had pointed at me. Oh, how I wanted to fling across the row and bop her one. They never called my name. So I assume they didn't think I was listening, or maybe they knew and just wanted to gloat.

"I'm not worried at all about losing Bam," Summer remarked. "But, that Lynzi girl should be. Hey, two more dates with him, maybe one more, and Bam Price is mine."

Starr leaned close to her cousin and asked, "Well, what did he tell you about his relationship with Lynzi?"

"Basically, you were right with what you told me about them. He's getting all he should need, BUT it's not enough," Summer said confidently. "He asked me if I could make him happy. My response was clear and simple. Having a taste of me will leave you never wanting another flavor again!"

"Go on then, Miss Kool Aid," Starr teased.

"See Cuz, you wrong," Summer laughed and said.

Starr inquired, "So when are you supposed to see him again?"

"Chile, I told him not to call me until he completely broke it off with that gal. You know I can't be sportin' other people's merchandise," Summer boasted. "I never borrow. Everything I USE is mine!"

They giggled. I quickly looked down my aisle to see if Lynzi had heard any of this. Luckily, she was gabbing away with Rain. I was glad. Even though I felt she needed to know how much of a dog Bam is, I didn't want my friend to find out that way.

It was weird. Practically none of us so-called "refined" girls were paying attention. I must admit the meeting was a tad boring. Mrs. Wright had been talking for a long while.

She continued, "Most of the functions will be held in the new year. However, we will be sponsoring a canned food drive for needy families around the holidays. There will be two workshops before Christmas, each on the second Saturday of the month, at noon. The first one is on finances and invest-ments. That will be held in this room, in November.

Girls started to yawn as she said, "December's workshop will be on careers. The location will be announced at a later date. New Year's Eve we're having a disco for you all."

Dymond uttered under her breath, "Disco? This ain't the seventies."

"The proceeds will pay for your pictures in the Ball pro-gram." Mrs. Wright took a deep breath and continued, "Now ladies, next year is when things get hectic. In January we have the Debutante Tea and social graces seminar. February is when we worship together at Mount Zion Baptist Church. Also, there is a personal grooming work-shop, and the pajama party."

Time was definitely running over because the manager of the hotel peeped his head into the room. That gesture made Mrs. Wright speed up. However, it was clear that she was not going to sit down until she finished.

She added, "March is when rehearsals start for the cotillion, every Tuesday and Thursday night till the ball. There will also be a forum that month. The topic is special concerns for young women. In April, there is a workshop on debutante manners, a visit to the retirement center, and a mother-debutante breakfast. And of course April first is the event the town is waiting for: the Ball!"

Finally in closing she said, "As you can see, our goal is to groom you ladies for greatness. We hope to help you become well-rounded individuals. Long-lasting friendships is something I'm sure you'll also gain. We've covered a lot of events, all of which will be explained in more detail later. I do hope your lunch was scrumptious, and that if nothing more, you enjoyed meeting the debs."

6

Buffing My Nails

I felt like such a terrible friend. It had been over a week now and I'd kept the news about Bam being unfaithful to myself. It's not like I didn't try on several occasions to tell Lynzi. However, pretty much every time I tried, she was too far in the denial state for me to spoil her imagined comfort.

Monday, on the way to school, I was about to spill the beans on Mr. Price, when Lynzi said, "Girrrl, every time I'm about to strike Bam out of my life, he steps up to bat and hits a home run! Payton, we had the best time together yesterday. He came over after church and we studied for the Lit midterm."

Sarcastically I uttered, "Gosh, that seems like so much fun."

"Now why you trippin'?" Lynzi voiced. "It's what we did to remember the material that proved to be both beneficial and fun."

"I won't ask for details," I stated with disinterest.

Lynzi gasped, "It was everything you could imagine, plus."

Oh, I wanted so bad to tell her about what Bam did Saturday night. Sure he was trying to get with her on Sunday, 'cause the day before the jerk tried with Summer and was turned down. I know this because Summer bragged about her date at church yesterday, without mentioning names. I knew who she was talking about. And anyway, as ruthless as Bam is, he probably would have tried to score with Lynzi even if he would have caught Summer in the end zone.

Another day, during cheerleading practice, I tried once again to alert my friend to the fact that her so-called boyfriend had another girl. But when we took our break, I saw Lynzi locked in a passionate embrace with Bam. I wanted to rush up to them and confront his tail, right there on the spot.

I was stopped dead in my tracks when Lynzi said, "Bam, I love you, so much. I don't know what my life would be like without you!"

"You don't have to ever worry about finding out," Bam breathed, as he came up for air from slobbing in Lynzi's ear.

Then Friday night, October 4, my birthday, on the way back to school from our away game in which we won twenty-one to three, I asked Lynzi to sit with me. Mind you, it wasn't because I just had to have her company. I again planned to spill the beans. But rudely, Lynzi irked my nerves with her arrogance.

"Sit with you," she said. "Chile, please! Just because you don't have a man to share a seat with doesn't mean I'm gonna neglect mine and babysit you. Honey, I don't think so."

Right then and there, I could have slapped her. Asking God to forgive me for the terrible thoughts helped me hold back. Luckily for her, I kept my cool, turned around, and headed for a seat alone.

During the ride I had time to replay Lynzi's comment again and again. The more I thought about it, the more I knew that her statement actually hurt me more than it made me angry. Dakari was sitting three rows ahead of me. Gosh, he looked so good. I always loved the way he cleaned up so nicely after a rainy, dirty game. Oh, how I wished things were the way they were last year. The two of us cuddled up in the back of the bus. Dakari and I loved away games. Whether we won or lost, knowing that we'd be together on the ride home was romantic.

I tried hard not to watch him. However, I found myself taken in by his every move. We had ceased speaking to each other. The fire had died. Secretly in parts of my heart the flame still burned brightly for him. Although, by my nonchalant actions, he would never know I still cared.

Most of the way home, Dakari slept. The drive was about an hour. During the two times that I noticed Dakari's eyes open, I so hoped he'd come and sit by me. I guess it's better that he never did, 'cause I have no clue what I would have said to him.

Staring at Dakari every second made the bus trip seem longer. So I was really glad when we finally pulled up to the school. A group of us had discussed going to the International House of Pancakes for a bite to eat. I was gonna crash. But, when Dakari announced that he was in, I quickly decided my bed could wait.

No one mentioned celebrating my seventeenth birthday. Since I was already so sad, that fact didn't bother me. It was just another day. Very rarely had the eight of us been together since school started, mostly because Dakari and I weren't together anymore. It's funny though, thinking back on all the good times we all shared together. Me and my three friend girls—Friend girls! I can't believe I said that. That is how my mother describes her girlfriends. Ironically, I tell her I hate that phrase, but now and again I catch myself using it.

The four of us girls, plus Dakari, Bam, Fatz who is Dymond's man, and Rain's boyfriend Tyson, who goes to T. W. Josey, called ourselves a "Gang." We joked around and said our name was, "Doe," and our colors were green and white. Well, all of us except Lynzi. See her favorite musicals are "Grease" and "Grease II." So, she loved to refer to us as the black T-Bird's and Pink Ladies. All the names are silly, I know. Gosh though, we sure had fun sharing, even the dumb stuff.

Dakari, Bam, Fatz, Lynzi, and I were all on the same bus. Dymond had to ride with the band. Rain didn't go to the game since it was away. She and Tyson were brushing up on their dating skills. They painted the town. Since this week was midterms, the two of them hadn't been out in a while.

When the five of us got off the bus, Dymond stood there waiting and yelled, "So, what's up? Ya'll tired, or are we on for somethin'?"

Her beau grabbed her around the waist and said, "Baby, I have taken the liberty of speaking for you. We have decided to enjoy each other's company and a meal at the IHOP."

It was funny to me, watching the two of them interact with each other. Here it was, this 4.0 senior talking like she was in the sixth grade and this 1.0 senior communicating like a Harvard grad. They seemed to be down with it, but it was perplexing to everyone else.

As I headed to my car, Rain and Tyson pulled up. I called them on my cellular phone to ask if they wanted to cut short their private time and join us. Rain didn't want to, but selfishly I pleaded. She gave in when I told her I needed her support. You know, since Dakari was going and all.

Getting my cellular phone was a struggle. As it was, I could only use it when I went out at night or on the weekends. Twisting my parents' arm for just that privilege was difficult.

I can remember my mother's words: "When I was your age the only thing I was given was a quarter to call home."

Once we got into it, when I reminded her that this wasn't her day and times had surely changed. She didn't budge on her position. However, when they heard of the unfortunate case of a girl from Jackson, South Carolina, who was assaulted while walking to get help after her car broke down, they changed their minds. I received a cellular phone that next day.

Conned by my friends into sitting beside me, Dakari spoke to me. It was the first time we'd said more than "Hello" to each other since the first day of school. He sure smelled divine! The strong, fresh scent almost enticed me to lean closer to him. Just as I was about to take a whiff, Dakari turned and looked me eye-to-eye. We all were so bunched in the booth that his sensual lips practically touched mine.

"So," he gasped, trying unsuccessfully to slide back and place distance between us, "it's been a while since we've sat this close. Shoot, Pay, so long that it kinda feels a little strange."

"Yeah, you're right," I lied, while deep inside thinking how marvelous it felt to be next to him.

Dakari complimented, "You know I never got to congratulate you on being our Homecoming Queen. You do our school proud. Even though my girl lost out, I'm sorta glad you won. I knew how much it meant to you."

Wow, he remembered our talk last Homecoming. We were at the dance and I recall just admiring the crowned Queen, Jacci Fielder. I told Dakari, while in his warm embrace on the dance floor, that I'd love to receive the title next year. I wondered if his remembering meant he still cared.

Before I could give thought to the answer he interrupted, "Payton, did you hear me?"

"Oh, I'm . . . sorry. Yes, I heard you I . . . I really appreciate your saying that," I rambled.

Fatz blurted out, "I hope you all are ready to give your order. I'm hungry as an ox. Where is our waitress? We've been sitting here for twenty minutes or so, and I'm about to go off in here."

"Man, chill out," Dakari argued. "It ain't been no twenty minutes. Plus, you see it's crowded in here. Yo' big butt can wait a second."

Fatz stood up and yelled, "Boy, don't make me go off on YOU! Your skinny tail needs to be tryin' to eat. Shoot."

Dymond pulled Fatz down 'cause it was clear that he was about to start fighting. When Fatz gets angry, he loses the proper English. Luckily, when he slammed to his seat, our server came. One good thing about the IHOP, it does not take long to get your food. In no time, we were all grubbin.'

Before we were totally done, we had visitors. Actually, while we were eating several folks stopped by our table and tried to be down. You know, like saying congrats to the guys for winning. One guy told Tyson that he couldn't wait to see him rule the courts this basketball season. A few girls stopped by to make small talk with us ladies, but the four of us knew they were just trying to peep the men. Not braggin', but we're known as the "90210 bunch" of Augusta, Georgia, better known as "29850."

Then just as we were paying the check, Starr and Summer stormed into the restaurant and headed directly for us. *What are they doing here,* I pondered? Suddenly it dawned on me; they probably had been driving all over town looking for Dakari and Bam.

Sadly, knowing that Dakari didn't have any more ties with me, I looked at Bam. Boy, was his tail squirming. Summer knew about Lynzi, but Lynzi didn't have a clue.

She was sitting on the other side of me.

She whispered, "Dag, I hate she's here. I feel sooo bad for you!"

To myself I breathed, "And I hate that the other 'she' is here. Boy, do I really feel bad for you."

"Dakari," Starr whined, "I have been searching everywhere for you, babe!"

He was sitting on the end, so Starr was able to place her hand on his cheek and kiss him. I overheard her quietly whisper something in regards to Bam. Then the two cousins that made me sick to my stomach said their goodbyes and left.

Not more than a minute later did Dakari say, "Well, folks, it's been real. Gotta go now though. Yo Bam, I need . . . I need to umm . . . holla at you. It's about some . . . game stuff. Can you roll?"

Bam breathed in a slick tone, "Ah, yeah man, that's— that's cool."

Lynzi pleaded, "Oh honey, do you have to go?"

"I would hang witcha, babe, but it's almost twelve and you gotta be home. Plus, my boy needs to rap to me. I'll call you first thang. Miss Payton, can you give my girl a ride home?" Bam nervously asked.

"Don't you worry about Lynzi. I'll see to it that she's just fine without you," I cautioned harshly.

He said, "Cool," never knowing that what I said had a deeper meaning.

As the two of them left, clearly henpecked, I decided to inform Lynzi all about Bam's infidelity. I couldn't allow him to make a fool of her anymore. She might get mad. She might not even believe me. Regardless of her response, I was determined to at least let her know.

When we pulled in front of Lynzi's home, she was silently in shock. However, I heard her thoughts loud and clear.

Even though this hadn't been the first time or the second, actually, that Bam had strayed, I knew my friend was devastated. Lynzi had grown to trust him once more, only to be betrayed again by the one she loved so dearly. Boy, could I relate. Regrettably, I too was without words.

So many things I knew I should tell her. Like, you'll get over him soon. This won't hurt so bad tomorrow. Or the classic response: He wasn't good enough for you anyway. My mind wanted to say all those things, only my tongue would not let those corny words roll from my mouth. Probably because I knew all too clearly that none of those statements would ease her pain.

For twelve minutes we just sat there. No music. No conversation. Nothing. Just two young women with broken hearts, trying desperately to mend each other with our presence alone.

At last I muttered, "Sweetie, I've got to get home. Believe me, I'm so sorry. That's the last thing I wanted to tell you. I've been battling with this for a while. Call me if you wanna talk. I love you, chick! Hang in there."

Saturday morning brought joy. I was about to be pampered. Twice a month, I went to Sasha's Place. It's a full-service salon. That day I had planned the works: full-body massage, relaxer in my hair, and acrylic on my nails.

Shirley, Tyson's mother, owns the shop. She named the place after her thirteen-year-old daughter, Sasha. Most of the stylists, including Shirley, are a stone trip! It is kind of a messy salon. But, boy, do they do good work! Sometimes I even get great advice.

"Ooh girlfriend, you're kinda tight around those shoulders. What problems you got?" Maxx the masseur asked as he pinched hard to relieve the stress.

I yelled, "Ouch, Maxx, that's too hard. It hurts!"

82

"Now, I'm trying very hard to work witcha," Maxx stated, pushing my head back down on the table. "Turn on back around and let me in on what's wrong."

Yeah, right, I thought to myself. Telling Maxx is like being on "Oprah"; the whole world would know. Dymond made that mistake once. Unfortunately, she told Maxx that she wasn't a virgin any longer. After that, every client he has that knows Dymond let her know that they knew. What a coincidence. Needless to say, after learning that he never heard my business.

"Since you being all quiet and stuff, let me just tell you. I already know about you and that fine Dakari breaking up. Don't be too down. You ain't the only one with man problems," he said in a caring voice.

OK, if he did hear my business, it would not be from me.

I questioned, "How'd you know about Lynzi and—"

"Chile—I don't know nothin' 'bout Lynzi. Shoot, I was talkin' 'bout me with the men problems," Maxx explained as he looked at me.

Now, I always thought he was soft, but gay? Let's just say I was uncertain. Dymond told me that he was. I guess I just did not want to believe her. Maxx puts you in the mind of Mario Van Peebles. I ask you, can you picture a gay Mario look-alike? Me neither! So, I had a very hard time digesting his comment. Before I cast judgment, I know that in God's eyes, a sin is a sin. Therefore, I won't throw a stone because he could throw one right back at me. I'm most certainly not perfect. However, out of love I wanted to help my brother out. Besides, he's too cute to sway.

When he took his hands off of me, I peeked up and said, "Maxx, you shouldn't like . . . date . . . I mean kiss. Shucks, you know what I'm sayin'," I babbled, hoping he'd get the point.

His response was hilarious, yet sad. He joked and said,

"The only thing a woman can do for me is point me to the nearest man." He later stated how some nights he wished he was straight. It was then, when he was most vulnerable, did I let him know that I'd be praying for him.

Next, I went up front to Shirley to get my hair laid. The shop was packed. And walking from the back to the front was no picnic. I might as well have been on a runway, 'cause all eyes were on me. It was uncomfortable. I promise, I had no clue what the fascination was. I mean, who am I?

"Why is everybody looking—no,—staring at me?" I asked Shirley.

She replied, as she applied my base, "Honey, those girls are just jealous. And don't say of what. You know a lot of these people aren't . . . well, let's just say, they are not as financially fortunate as you are. And what kills me is that they scrape together money to get their hair done, and yet they won't help their mamas with the bills."

I could only say, "Gosh!"

One thing I liked about Mrs. Graham, Dakari's mom, is that she was cool.

When we were dating, she never gave me drama. Actually, she called me to offer comfort when she learned that Dakari and I had split. In a small way, it made me feel better to know that I was her choice for him. Too bad it wasn't her choice to make.

But Miss Shirley, boy, did she and Rain have a hard time getting along! I don't think it was Rain personally, but she probably would be equally rude to any girl Tyson dates seriously. If you ask me, I think she's too attached to her son and needs to find a man. But who ever asks me? Miss Shirley knows that Rain is my best friend, yet she still tried me and talked about her.

She spoke up as she blow dried my hair, "You know, Payton, I'm a little disappointed in your buddy Rain."

I didn't know what she was going to say. I was silent.

Rain is the sweetest person I know. Therefore, if she did happen to do something wrong, I knew it wasn't to be spiteful.

Miss Shirley continued, "Rain called my house at one o'clock in the morning. Now, that's just plain inexcus—"

I interrupted and said, "She probably wanted to make certain that Tyson got home OK. I'm sure she didn't mean any disrespect."

Obviously, my reasoning didn't sit too well with her, because she kept on blasting my best friend. Finally, I told her that I didn't want to hear anymore. As she kept on anyway, I wondered why I continued coming here. When I looked in the mirror and saw my gorgeous hairstyle, I knew.

Billie did my nails. She is a forty-six-year-old woman, and her daughter is twenty. Like Miss Shirley, she also has no husband. Her man passed away five years ago. She's such a kindhearted lady. Very easy to talk to. Miss Billie is the nicest one in the salon.

"So, you aren't over him yet, huh?" Billie asked as she slid the emery board across, up and down.

I murmured in exasperation, "It's so hard!"

"Well," Billie counseled, "getting over a guy is just like buffing your nails. When you first sat down they were tore up. And in comparison, your situation is tore up. Broken heart, broken nail. Same thing. It takes time to correct the problem. You must smooth over the rough edges. The more you work to get him out of your mind, the sooner it will actually happen."

I was quiet, soaking in her every word. Deep down, I felt God sent her to speak to me.

She said, "Look at me; I'm filing and cutting your nails down. You must do the same when it comes to living without this guy in your life. Cut out thinking of him constantly. Sand down the memories. Honey, you have too much going for you. Trust me, he'll be back. But when he comes, flash your beautiful polished nails in his face. Chile, you know what I'm sayin.' Tell that joker to talk to the hand. After all this hard work, there is an end result. And it is worth it."

I started to feel good. Every time I talked to Miss Billie I seemed better. I guess it's her wisdom.

"No more broken nails, just pretty ones. And so should it be when you are done mending your heart. You'll be able to live without him. Your heart will be shiny and new, just like your nails," she consoled.

"Wow," I expressed with hope in my voice, "I understand. Getting over Dakari takes work. And I'm going to keep working on keeping him out of my system.

"Yep, it's just like buffing my nails."

7

Learning
the Campus

$\mathcal{J}$ couldn't believe it would be Halloween this weekend.
Time was flying so quickly. Seemed like only yesterday
it was August and now . . . well, now the leaves, as well as
the temperature, were falling.

It was Tuesday afternoon and I had just gotten home
from a long day at school. I was just about to do my home-
work when the phone rang. I knew it was Rain asking if I'd
scoop her up for the debutante meeting. Tonight we were
voting on the gown we'd wear at the cotillion. This would
be the first year that we'd all be dressed alike. Supposedly
in the past, folks were spending too much money to outdo
each other. My mom said some girls purchased wedding
gowns. To me that's a bit much.

"Yes Rain," I said impatiently into the receiver.

"Hello . . . Payton," the unknown female voice said with
uncertainty.

I replied, "This is she. Who am I speaking to?"

"Well, I'm not Rain," she laughed. "I hope you remember

me. This is Hayli Woodruff . . . you know, Drake Graham's girlfriend, from the University of Georgia."

Embarrassed, I said, "Oh, oh Hayli, I'm so sorry. Of course, I know who you are. I just assumed it was my best friend."

"That's no problem," she responded in a sweet tone. "Mrs. Graham gave me your number. I hope that's all right."

Quickly I answered, "Sure, that's fine. What can I do for you?"

"First of all, I apologize for calling last minute. Please know that I've been meaning to give you a ring for weeks. I've just been swamped with organizing this weekend's minority recruiting visit. Did you receive any literature on it?" she asked.

I admitted, "Yes I did, but we have a game this weekend. To be honest, I didn't give it much thought."

Hayli pried, "Isn't your game on Friday?"

"Yes it is," I informed her.

"Well, that's one of the reasons I've been meaning to call. You see we've sort of changed things around. Most of the events are on Saturday and early Sunday morning. This way most students will not have to miss their football games," Hayli said.

"That's nice," I commented. "Actually, that kinda changes things."

"Oh Payton, I hope so. Being Director of Minority Recruitment is a big deal to me. I really want to see more of us at Georgia. Right now we only make up a small proportion of the population. And believe me, we're trying to raise our numbers," she said, almost angrily.

Hayli went on to explain that she devised a plan that she hoped would attract and retain more black high school seniors. Her idea was actually pretty fascinating. With the help of the registrar's office, her committee gathered a list of the top black applicants. They asked them to personally come to the recruitment weekend and bring friends that might also be interested in the University of Georgia.

Upon their arrival, they would be paired with a current UGA student that would show them around. In addition, the high school senior would be housed for the weekend with that Georgia student. After Hayli relayed that information, she asked me something.

"So, I was surely hoping you'd like to hang with me this weekend and be my recruit," Hayli uttered, anticipating a positive response.

I murmured, "To be honest, Hayli, I only applied to UG because I thought Dakari was going there. And . . . well, now that we've broken up, I'm kinda steering away from your school."

"Honey, I hear ya! Buuut . . . let me just say there's a lot more to college than chasing a man. I know you know that. Being real, though, I will say that since that is a large part of our nature, let me assure you that we've got plenty of fine, smart, and sweet guys around our campus!" Hayli exclaimed.

I cautioned, "Well . . . "

"Don't say no just yet. Talk it over with your parents and ask a few girlfriends if they'd like to accompany you. Just to let you know, I live in an apartment with three friends. All four of us have our own room, so no one will be uncomfortable. My number is 706-555-3142. Call me and let me know your decision. We'd truly love to show you guys a great time," Hayli invited.

All during the ride to the meeting, the four of us discussed the trip. Two were for and two were against. Dymond was set on going to Howard undergrad, then Harvard Medical School. She called it her first-class ticket out of the ghetto. Howard had already accepted her. However, they haven't talked scholarship money, so she's

89

not one hundred percent locked in.

Rain has got serious tradition on her side. Her great-grandmother, grandmother, mother, and aunt all went to Spelman College in Atlanta. She's been bred to be the fourth generation to attend. I know if she goes there, she'll have it made. There's too much history there for Rain to fail. I hear they take care of their own. And Rain has got to be theirs, if her great-grandmother went there.

Lynzi and I weren't so set with our college decision. So the two of us thought that the weekend could be both educational and exciting. Lynzi and I tried hard to persuade them to at least check out the school.

Dymond insisted, "I'm not tryin' to go to no school in the South. Come June, I will be laboring hard to get away from these backwards people. I'm headed straight up. Yeah, the North, baby!"

"It's only a day and a half," I tried to entice her. "And Dy, there is a party Saturday night. Now, a college bash? I know you can't resist it."

"OK, OK, don't twist my arm. Since you put it that way . . . count me in," Dymond announced with a smile on her face.

The deb meeting was way more intense than I expected. Girls bickered back and forth over whose selection should be chosen as the design we'd wear. I personally didn't place too much merit in it. I mean, as long as the dumb dress would be flattering to my size-six figure, any selection was OK by me.

However, that was a big problem with most girls. Some wanted a tight look, and others preferred a loose style. Ironically, Dymond, who was one of the heavier girls, made the biggest stink about having the short-tight dress. No one, not even me, and I've been her friend for years, could figure out why she wanted that particular type. Though, I will admit she's the cutest size twelve I've ever seen in a mini-skirt.

Since we could not reach an agreement unanimously, the decision was put to a vote. We all wrote down our first and second choices. My mother collected the ballots and announced that the selected gown would be revealed at our next meeting.

The week just flew by like a Lear Jet. Our game got canceled due to stormy weather. So, with permission from our folks, the four of us headed to Athens. In the car we piled munchies, sleeping bags, compact discs, and a radar detector. Of course, my parents didn't know I had one. I didn't even intend to speed. I just had it handy to alert me to "the man." You know, just in case I happened to be blabbing at the mouth instead of paying attention and maybe, just maybe, my foot pressed too hard on the pedal. Although . . . most of the time I use cruise control!

We left shortly after school, four young ladies heading for a world we knew nothing about. I think we all had expectations.

Rain wanted to one day pledge Alpha Kappa Alpha. Since Hayli and one of her three roommates were in this sorority, Rain felt that this was a great opportunity to accumulate pointers on their style. Really, she wanted to peep them for information on how they select their pledges.

Dymond, on the other hand, wanted to do some networking. The speaker for the brunch on Sunday was Dr. Sheryl Brickhouse. This lady has her own successful obstetrics and gynecology practice in Washington, D.C. Dr. Brickhouse attended Harvard Medical School and was one of the first African-American students to be enrolled at Georgia. Dymond professed that she and this doctor had a lot in common, being that Dy wanted to one day deliver babies, dreamed of attending the historically black university located in our nation's capital, and lived for a Harvard Medical School degree. Forget the party; her mission was to meet this lady.

Since it had only been a week since Lynzi gave Bam the boot, the whole ordeal still weighed heavily on her mind. She insanely believed the only way she'd get over him was to have sex with a college guy. Her plan was to give it up to the first guy she slow-dragged with. I suppose Lynzi assumed this act of impulsiveness would allow her to feel irresistible, sexy, and wanted—the three things that Bam snatched away when he decided she wasn't enough to satisfy him.

All of us tried to tell Lynzi that her plan was ludicrous. We reasoned that sex would not give her the validity and comfort that she was so desperately searching for. However, she was determined to carry out her mission. Secretly, I just prayed her plan would fail.

And for me, I just wanted peace. I expected to have a weekend free from thoughts of Dakari. Somewhere along the way, God had placed a small desire in my broken heart to mend. A small part of me wanted to move on. I hoped this weekend would help me do just that. I planned to enjoy the adventure with my best buddies, meet new people, and press towards a bright future.

"Well, hello," Hayli said smiling from ear to ear. "I am so glad you all made it. Why don't I show you inside and introduce you to my suite mates. We have about an hour before the mixer."

Lynzi blabbed as we walked into the beautifully decorated three story condo, "A mixer . . . yeah, that sounds cool. I'm sure guys are gonna be there, huh? I mean, what's it all about?"

Hayli laughed a tad and said, "Oh sure! Guys, girls, professors, and community leaders will be in attendance. All in an effort to attract you to Georgia. We won't have to eat here because there will be hors d'oeuvres and pop at the event. Also, the Alpha Phi Alpha jazz band will be playing. They're grrreat! Not to sound like Kelloggs' Tony the Tiger, but there's just no other way to adequately describe them. Afterwards, my roommates and I are planning a little gab session with you guys. We'll stay up till dawn if the conversation gets intense. Just remember there's a big day tomorrow."

"Thanks for having us stay here. Your place is gorgeous. Plus, this really gives us a chance to see what college life is all about," I humbly stated.

After we freshened up, we met the girls. It was great that we all got along nicely. I hoped that it would last all weekend. With eight black women under one roof, you never know when to expect a blowup.

The layout of their pad was nice. Two bedrooms upstairs with a full bath and two bedrooms downstairs with a full bath. On the middle level was the entry, kitchen, nook, den, powder room, laundry, and deck.

Rent is twelve hundred a month. Food and utility run them around a hundred dollars. Don't forget miscellaneous costs. Shucks, that's over four hundred dollars a month. Gosh, I wondered what their parents did. Hey, maybe scholarship money was paying for this. However, whatever, I know that this is the way I want to live. No parents, no dorm mother, no curfews—what a life!

When we got to the mixer, the four of us went our separate ways. Hayli and her sorority sisters had Rain with them. I believed they adored the fact that she dreamed of one day wearing pastel pink and mint green. Lynzi was mad that Rain got to meet all those cute Alphas in the jazz ensemble.

Now, Dymond was all over the place. She searched here and there for Dr. Brickhouse. Dy said she needed every advantage to meet and know the lady that could one day write her letter of recommendation to Harvard. My mouth told her jokingly that she was crazy, but my brain knew she was smart.

Lynzi was busy guy hopping. There were three questions she asked. If she received any wrong answers, Lynzi quickly moved on to the next target. Are you in college? Do you play sports? And is there a girlfriend in your life? These are the items she wanted to hear yes to. Isn't it sad that, when some people get burned in a monogamous relationship, they look to destroy other people? That's exactly why the dating world is so messed up. Standards are so low. People accept and do anything.

I was pretty laid back. Just enjoying watching my friends do their thang. Sitting all alone in a corner with the company of a hot wing and cherry coke. I would have been content to stay that way all night. However, my space was invaded by a slightly familiar, comfortable-toned voice.

"Remember me?" the voice uttered.

As my eyes moved up the body of the gentleman in front of me, I said, "Should I?"

He responded softly, "Come on. Even though I only had the pleasure of meeting you once, it wasn't that long ago. And I haven't forgotten you!"

Oh my gosh, I thought with pleasure when I dawned on his face. It was Tad Taylor, still tall, dark, and as handsome as ever. Yep, that's the guy I met at the first Georgia football game. Dakari introduced us. If my memory serves me correctly, he wasn't too fond of Tad. Hey, that's all the more reason to like this guy from South Carolina.

"Tad," I said in a surprised tone, "how are you?"

He joked, "Oh, so you do remember me?"

As I shook my head yes, Tad added, "Well, then I guess

I'm the lucky one."

He then sat down beside me and the two of us chatted for the duration of the function. This dude was so nice. Of course, he just had to ask about Dakari. He didn't seem that pleased to hear of Dakari's success on the field. I guess it's that rivalry thang. Fortunately, he did crack a slight smile when I mentioned Dakari and I were no longer an item.

Our conversation, though extensive, was not intense. We were justa laughin.' I had no expectations from the relationship we were forming. I just enjoyed the moment.

Through listening to him, I found out quite a bit about this intriguing fella. First of all, his year was going just as great, football-wise, as Dakari's. Actually, he was the top rusher in the state of South Carolina. When I asked him about his grades, he gave me a smirk. Two point eight nine is what he said. Not great, but certainly acceptable.

We talked about our dreams. I went on and on about how I want this and need to accomplish that. Even though he looked at me with interest, he must've thought I was shallow. 'Cause when Tad spoke of his dream, I was blown away.

"My dream, or should I say goal, is to live a life that pleases God. You know, Payton, if I please Him then it doesn't matter who I displease. However, if I displease God, then frankly, it doesn't matter who I please," he declared.

When the evening drew to a close, we said a simple goodbye. Like a gentleman, he escorted me to my friends. Of course, they were all smiling. Although I didn't express or say it, I so hoped to run into him again before the weekend was done.

At the apartment, we stayed up awhile. They all cornered me on Tad. My comments on him were evasive. So, since I wasn't giving up any business, they switched the

95

conversation to a general discussion on the same topic. MEN!

Later, in Hayli's room, the two of us gabbed even more. She confessed that Drake had told her why Dakari broke it off with me. I was truly touched when she put in her two cents.

"You know, Payton, I'm glad you didn't give in to Dakari sexually. Let me tell you from experience, if he left you because he wanted some, then believe me chances are when he would have gotten some, he would have left anyway. My roommates and I were talking just the other day about our regrets in life. And the one thing that we all regretted was that our virginity was gone. Having sex with a guy doesn't make things easier, or really better. Trust me, stuff just gets more complicated. And if it makes you feel any better, Dakari's mom detests that new girl," Hayli expressed as she chuckled.

Saturday was one of those days when the phrase "Boy, time flies when you're having fun" really applies! My friends and I were truly enjoying ourselves. Hayli left early to organize the day's activities. Her roommates cooked us breakfast. Tasting their pancakes, eggs, and bacon let me know that I'd better take lessons from my mom, so that next year when I'm on my own, my food will be edible. Don't get me wrong. The meal they prepared wasn't burnt. Unfortunately for my stomach, it was close. Dymond, who could throw down in a kitchen, offered to make them breakfast on Sunday.

The game was great! Well, except I didn't see Tad anywhere. Not that I was looking for him or anything. Yeah right, who am I kidding? Finally, when I didn't spot him, I realized that he was probably sitting in the recruiting section again.

The exhibition followed the game. I felt it was pretty interesting. Professors were at different booths answering questions about the University of Georgia and different majors. Hayli was mingling. I must say, she is the perfect hostess. Her warm demeanor alone made most of us strongly consider attending the school.

I had about as much an idea of what I wanted to major in as a rookie cop does in trying to solve a murder case. No clue! My father wanted me to major in business, of course, so that I could one day run his dealership. My mother, though, wasn't really pushing me hard in that direction. Probably because she hoped that my brother, Perry, would take over. So since I was indecisive, I took advantage of the information and talked with quite a few deans. By day's end, I had acquired lots of literature to aid in my decision.

Boy was this weekend moving too quickly. It was already Sunday morning. We were at the school café for the brunch. The dance the night before was the popular topic of dialogue. We had a blast! The college students in attendance were so friendly. They made us feel . . . kinda at home. Luckily, we were not treated like a bunch of babies that they had to spoon-feed. We were all on the same level, enjoying the night.

Tad, regrettably, missed all the action. He was not there. At first I was disappointed, then I realized that fate was not on our side. I mean, how would it ever work? I can't give my whole heart away, if it's still mending.

Oddly enough, right before the speaker gave her message, Tad found his way to our table. My friends immediately looked pleased. I didn't mean to be rude, but it was the only way I knew to ward off my emotions from getting all riled up again.

"Hello, ladies," he kindly said to my friends and me.

Tad seemed a bit nervous. Part of me thought it was

cute. Then with confidence, he looked directly at me and asked for my phone number.

I stupidly said, "I'm sorry, Tad, but I think it's best that we not be friends. Casual acquaintances are fine. Therefore, my phone number won't be necessary."

At that point, I got kicked in both shins. One by Rain on the left. The other kick was given by Lynzi on the right.

"Oh, please forgive me," he conceded reluctantly, "for being too forward."

Before Tad could walk away, Dymond stood up with a piece of paper in her hand and insisted, "She was just joking. Here's her digits. She has her own line. So, feel free to use it . . . soon!"

Dr. Brickhouse was most inspiring. She really didn't lecture; she encouraged. I wish I had taped it to be played in the future, when I needed a boost.

She charged, "Life is a game. You must play to win. Don't be a hare in the race with a tortoise, slacking off because you think you have the game licked. No, no, you must strive to always execute the skills God has bestowed upon you. Remember this: 'What you give will grow, and what you keep you'll lose.' Yep, lose just like the hare who stopped in the middle of the race because he had outjudged his opponent."

As I sipped my water, I noticed that she had everyone's attention. This intellectual woman had come down on our level. And her positive words seemed to be sticking.

"Do not underestimate," Dr. Brickhouse continued, "what you can receive next year in college. For even the smallest lessons will prove beneficial once you enter the real world. Study your courses! Study your teachers! Study your fellow students! Study your dorm! Even study the extracurricular activities! Some of you may think it's a bit far-fetched. However, trust me when I say college is meant to help you step up to the game of life. Note, next year in whatever school you may attend, that being successful in college is more than learning your major. To fully get the most out of the experience, keep in mind, it's learning the campus!"

8

Expecting...
Maybe... Baby...

*Y*ou know, it's weird! I had waited all my life to be a senior in high school, and it seemed like it would never come. Shucks, now that it was finally here, my twelfth-grade year is fading fast, more and more each day. Just another reminder that time is precious. The last thing I want, come June, is regrets.

Dakari and I have been able to finally be kind to one another. Everyone who predicted that he and Starr would be broken up by Halloween was way off the mark. The two of them seemed as close as peanut butter and jelly on a sandwich. And you know how tight they stick together.

Unfortunately, I'm still battling my feelings. I've come to the conclusion, though, that a part of me will always love him. However, I just accept the fact that it is what it is and press on.

Two nights ago, Starr called me at home. To this day, I still haven't been able to figure out what the point of her call was. It was weird. She was direct, yet very evasive at the same time.

"So, I hear you haven't found a date to the ball yet. I know several guys that—" Starr voiced without my wanting or asking for her input.

I cut her off and said, "What do you care? No, as a matter of fact, I don't want to know why you're interested."

"Don't get upset, Payton," Starr uttered with fake concern. "I was just trying to help you out of a desperate situation. Anyway, moving on . . . have you spoken with Kari lately?"

Now for her to be asking me that question, there must be some tension. My mother always told me that what looks good on the outside isn't always as it appears. Yet, I didn't pry. I simply kept my distance and ended the conversation.

Lots of Christians I know don't celebrate Halloween. Even my parents have changed their tune on the holiday. See, when Perry and I were six and four, our folks let us dress up and trick-or-treat. About two years after that, their tune switched. Not only did they feel it was getting dangerous, but they said there was no way that they'd, in good conscience, allow their children to celebrate an evil holiday.

Of course, as children you just can't take away candy and costumes and expect us to understand. Luckily, the church intervened with a magnificent solution. Every October 31, there is a big dress-up bash for young adults, called Hallelujah Night. Contrary to the usual theme, this party has a twist. Everyone wears outfits like a character from the Bible. Before chattering, playing games, and digging into the refreshments, we each say who our character is and give a brief account of his or her biblical history.

This year, I was Mary, Martha and Lazarus's sister. My costume was so fun to put together. Bunches of sheets from the hall closet, tied and hung all over me.

"Why'd you choose Mary?" my Sunday school teacher asked me.

I stood over the group and humbly replied, "Well, I wanted to portray someone who I truly aspire to be like. And when I read Luke 10:38–42, where Mary of Bethany sat at Jesus' feet, clinging to His every word, I get excited! I say excited because she's like a sponge, absorbing all her body could hold. At that moment, nothing else is relevant. Her only concern is hearing the Savior speak. I want to be like that. I need to be like that. Mary forgot the entertaining. She put aside the serving. This holy woman didn't touch a dish. I know that if I focus half that much on my daily walk with God, my life would be a lot easier."

———————————————

There were about thirty people there. Everyone had talked about their outfit except Lynzi. She kept disappearing. One minute she was beside me, then the next second she'd be gone. Lastly, after everyone had spoken, she stood up and made a comment.

Lynzi, full of emotion, said, "I chose the adulterous woman."

I was shocked when I viewed her outfit. She kept her coat on until she spoke. When she pulled it off, holes and dirt were all over her rangy costume. It looked like she hadn't changed in months.

As a tear trickled down her face she continued, "I'm so full of sin. I need God to forgive me like He did this woman. I've sinned!"

She dashed out of the room and I followed her. Although we hadn't talked in a while, I couldn't imagine what would be making her so upset. I searched everywhere and couldn't find her. I caught up with her in the nursery. She was weeping over the crib.

I placed my arm around her and said, "What's wrong?"

She held back her tears and said nothing. Lynzi sharply turned and moved to the other side of the room. It was crystal clear that she was in pain. I tried again to get her to open up.

"Lynzi," I voiced while walking closer to her, "you know you can tell me anything. I love you and care deeply about everything in your life. Whatever is bothering you, together we can fix it. Open up to me, pleeease, Lynzi!"

She blurted out, "I'm pregnant, OK? There, I said it. Are you happy? Now leave me alone."

Lynzi tried to walk out the door. I blocked it. She reached to push me out of the way.

I begged, "Let me talk to you. You can't just say something like that and try to leave."

"Payton, please don't tell anybody. I'll never forgive you if you do," Lynzi spoke with a strong voice and a stern face.

"Talk to me . . . talk. I won't say nothin.' You gotta know I won't," I replied.

My sad friend began to open up as she plopped down on the chair next to the changing table. "Well, you know . . . umm . . . Bam and I aren't even together anymore, right?"

I nodded my head in agreement, holding my breath in anticipation of what was to come. I was tired of wondering what, why, who, how. OK, maybe I knew how.

"My period hasn't come on and I'm a few days late," Lynzi said. "And I went and got a pregnancy test. Shoot, I got five pregnancy tests. They were in the same box. I took three of them and they all came back positive. I don't know what I'm gonna do. My mom will kill me."

She paused. She sobbed. She moaned.

Then she continued, "He's with somebody else. I do still love him though. But . . . but, we're just kids. We surely can't have a kid. This is crazy! Oh God, I'm so sorry. Lord, I'm so sorry. I'm so sorry!"

It was hard seeing my buddy in utter despair, crying out to God for forgiveness from sin. I guess this is one reason why the Lord doesn't want us to fornicate. You know, 'cause when we do, this is a classic example of the mess we get in. Oh yeah, it does feel good when you're in the moment of passion. Then everything is great. Obviously, this is not how God intended it to be.

She's right. My friend is just a teenager. Lynzi's seventeen years old. How can she have a baby? How can any high school girl carry that type of burden?

I went over to her and wiped some of her tears away. I held her as close as I could. Her pain was mine. My heart was breaking, yet I was so glad it wasn't me. Only a few months ago, I was willing to give Dakari everything. Every part of me. Every inch of me. Just so he'd stay with me. This could have been my end result. I could have become pregnant!

What's worse is the fact that Dakari still probably would have broken up with me anyway. I'm trying to go to college. Full-time mom is not what I want to major in.

"Lynzi," I softly said, "we're gonna fix this. Some way we'll make this better. Don't ask me how. Right now, I have no answers. Just trust me, we'll get things back on track."

"Please help me, Payton. Help me. I don't know what to do," Lynzi cried.

That night I tossed and turned for hours. I was trying to find a way that Lynzi could get out of this mess. My friend is pregnant! The very thought gave me chills.

And Bam, her two-timing ex-boyfriend, had no idea of his new responsibility. He's off gallivanting, trying to get with some other girl. Now isn't that crazy? Hope she doesn't end up pregnant too.

When stuff like this happens, I wonder why we girls stress ourselves to date these jerks. Why do we fantasize about them? Why are we always up in their faces? Shucks, we make ourselves available to their every call. We bend over backwards to please them, only to be let down in the end.

I want so bad to talk to my mom about this. But . . . you know, I say, "I have a friend who is pregnant," and she'll automatically assume it's me. Who really ever believes the "I have a friend" story?

But this time, I do have a friend. The question is, how can I get my mom to believe it? She knows that I've been upset for a while. I just bet if I share this, she'll jump to the wrong conclusion. That settles that. I can't talk to her.

Why is my phone ringing at this hour. It's almost midnight. I hurried, grabbed the phone and said, "Who's trying to get me in trouble?"

"Hey Pay, it's me," Lynzi said, sounding a little better.

"Well, I sure haven't gotten you off my mind," I responded.

Lynzi voiced, "I'm feeling OK."

"What do you mean?" I asked.

"Because," she said taking a deep breath, "I thought about this thing and I got a solution."

"A solution?" I questioned.

Lynzi abruptly announced, "I'm going to have an abortion."

An abortion? I just knew I didn't hear her right. No way is that what she said. My buddy could never kill anyone.

OK, true enough, I did pass the thought of killing myself a few months ago. But when I thought it all out, I was just joking. Lynzi is too scared to squash a fly. She says the fly's spirit will haunt her forever. Therefore, I just know she'd never be able to handle killing her own flesh and blood.

She broke the silence and asserted, "Payton, did you hear me? I wanna get rid of this thing."

"This thing? this thing? Are you crazy!" I yelled. "Lynzi, how can you ever think of taking someone else's life?"

"It's easy enough for you to be so condescending. Just think about it," Lynzi started, "it's not your baby. You're not the one that's having a baby. You're not the poor little pregnant girl. What if it were you? Just imagine, Miss Perfect, if you were having Dakari's baby. Now remember, you dread to tell him because he dumped you for someone else. Seriously, ask yourself, what would you do?"

Little did she know I had already asked myself that question time and time again. No answer came to mind, though. I was like a block of ice stored in the back of the freezer for weeks, frozen solid. I couldn't thaw myself out to think how I'd react if I were her.

Lynzi proceeded, plainly distraught. "OK, Payton, since you can't give me an answer, maybe hearing it told that way makes you more sympathetic to what I'm going through. The option of giving the baby up for adoption isn't appealing."

Why not? That may be your best option, I thought. This way both Lynzi and the baby would benefit.

She explained, "For one, I'd have to actually give birth. I'm not tryin' to be selfish, but then the world would know I was pregnant. Secondly, the child would more than likely be scarred—you know, from not having its real mom and dad. Worst of all, the parents could be horrible people. Don't even tell me that I could pick the people myself. Shucks, even though that is an option, those couples are on their best behavior. Just my luck, I'd choose the wrong couple. I can see it now. Twenty years down the road, this baby would come, track me down, and blame me for everything that's wrong in his or her life."

Lynzi finally hushed up. She burst into tears. I tried to calm her down.

"Adoption isn't as bad as you make it seem," I gently expressed to her.

Even though I uttered those positive words, deep inside my soul I kinda felt she had a point. I just couldn't let Lynzi know I felt that way. There was no way honesty would be a good thing in this situation. Even though my friend wouldn't know how I felt, at least I could be truthful to myself. So, in silent conclusion, I guess you could say, I thawed out. For it was evident to me that if it were me I'd probably . . . more than likely. . . definitely . . . terminate too.

How dare I judge her so harshly? Who am I to condemn her? At that moment, I thought of the One who could. God. Without thinking on it too hard, my gut told me He would not approve. So, with absence of my opinion, I told Lynzi what was best. That is, what God expects us to do.

"Lynzi, you go to the same church I do. We hear the same messages. The two of us serve the same, the only, God. Now don't misunderstand me; I'm not trying to preach or get all biblical or anything, but isn't God against this? I don't really know exactly what the Bible says on this issue. However, I will find out," I promised.

"Payton!" Lynzi shouted harshly, "I thought we discussed earlier that this information is not to be shared with anyone?"

"Well, this whole situation is getting to me. But, hey, I gave you my word. So count on me to keep this to myself. Surely you do not want to hear this, but, because I love you, you're gonna hear it anyway. Lyn, you need to tell Bam as soon as possible. Let's be honest. This is his baby too. Isn't it?" I questioned.

"Of course, Payton. With all that I'm dealing with, I can't believe you went THERE! I'll decide when to tell him, OK?" Lynzi snapped. "Just let me do it my own way, in my own time."

All week, Lynzi wasn't the same. My vibrant, fun-filled, living-life-to-the-fullest friend was just the opposite. It was eerie. She wasn't even eating like she used to. Only one meal a day, sometimes. And that was only those Slim Fast cans.

Trying to justify her actions she moaned, "Certainly I can't eat because I'm putting on weight being pregnant. I've got to stay slender, so that no one can tell."

Even though her rationale kinda made sense, it was so stupid. I couldn't tell her that because then she'd alienate me too. It was crucial that I allow her to confide in me with what she was doing. God forbid she'd faint during cheer-leading practice. Shoot, if something like that happened, at least I'd be able to explain to the medical examiner her every move.

I too was getting weary. At night this awful predicament was causing me to lose sleep. I'd try to count sheep, but all I could think on was Lynzi and her plight. So I prayed, and that always seemed to make me feel better.

"Lord, I don't know what to say. I'm not praying for myself. I need to ask You to help my comrade. I know You're a miracle worker. I have always been told that by my family, and Lord, I believe that from the depths of my soul. If there is any possibility that You can make this mess turn out OK, please do it," I uttered on my knees with hope.

It was a dreary, wet day when Lynzi called me over to her place. I didn't have a clue what she wanted, but I felt yucky driving all the way there. Probably because I knew whatever she wanted to discuss would depress me. How ironic—my mood matched the weather.

"What took you so long, girl?" Lynzi voiced anxiously, while snatching me in the house.

"Quit pulling me! I got here as fast as I could. You wouldn't tell me over the phone what this is all about. So, it couldn't be that impor—"

"Oh, hush up," Lynzi mandated as she cut me off.

She was busy, cleaning some of everything. My girl-friend dashed from the kitchen, to the bathrooms, to the den. You would have thought someone had spun me around and around, as dizzy as I felt from watching my busy buddy.

I finally yelled, "Lynzi, what is wrong with you?"

"I've decided to do what you've been bugging me to do all week," Lynzi quickly blurted out, as she ran past me spraying some of her mom's old perfume through the house.

What was she talking about? I had no clue. Realistically, there were several things I had been on her to do. Eat, talk with our pastor, confirm this pregnancy with her doctor, pray and—

Before I could finish that thought, I heard a car door slam. Peeping out the window, I was surprised to see who I saw. Looked like Lynzi was about to do the one other thing I was just about to ponder: tell Bam.

I should have known something like this was up. Lynzi cleaning? She hates cleaning. She'd rather leave the ring around her bathtub and still bathe in it than clean. Luckily, her mother doesn't allow such laziness. Now, I got it. This is all for Bam.

"Alright, I'm gonna sit here. Payton, you get the door," bossed Lynzi.

The stupid boy rang the door repeatedly, tryin' to be funny. Just ignorant. As I walked to open it, I wondered why I was here at all. This should be a private moment between them.

Lynzi voiced in the back of me, "I'm so nervous."

"It'll be OK," I replied, but really not so sure myself how he'd react.

The three of us had been sitting around for about fifteen minutes. We were just shootin' the breeze. I thought maybe Lynzi was waiting for me to excuse myself. She would then be able to break the news. Surely that was it. She wanted me for moral support.

"Well, let me leave you two alone," I said as I got up to walk out of the room.

Lynzi stood up also and asserted, "Oh no, Payton! You can't leave. Don't you have something to tell Bam?"

"I do?" I questioned, looking at her like she was crazy.

Bam divulged, "Ah yeah, Miss Lady, my girl told me that you had to drop somethin' on me. What's up?"

You should have seen Lynzi's eyes. She was so pitiful. I couldn't believe she actually wanted me to tell him. I reasoned that he'd probably go off on us both. It's true that I wanted to help Lynzi through this, but telling Bam that he's probably a father is way more involved than I needed to be.

I sat back down, took a very deep breath, and told Bam everything. There was a long pause. The room was so still that I could count the number of raindrops falling outside.

Finally, Bam spoke. Surprisingly, he was subdued. He went over to Lynzi.

Touching her stomach, he sputtered in a partial daze, "Expecting . . . maybe . . . baby?"

9

Testing Our Friendship

*H*ow dare you betray me like that. Just think, I had the nerve to think you were my friend. Well, I'm dumb no more. Us being close—that's over," Lynzi hastily said to me.

I was shocked. What in the world brought this on? Even though I hadn't spoken to her since we—no, since I—told Bam when I left the two of them that day, we were fine. How that changed in a couple of days is anybody's guess.

The friendship Lynzi and I have has been like the stock market: up one day, then down the next day without warning. So in some ways her weird reaction, though odd, didn't surprise me too much.

I questioned with the utmost sincerity, "Lynzi, I don't understand where this anger is coming from. Why are you trippin'? The other day we were the best of friends, and now you stand here and say I betrayed you. What's this really all about?"

"Oh Payton Skky," Lynzi uttered even madder than she was before, "don't play dumb. You know what you did. So don't act all innocent and stuff. What's the sayin'? With friends like you, I don't need—"

Abruptly, I cut her off and said, "I'm not your enemy, Lynzi. For weeks I've been going through turmoil because of your pain. Some nights I haven't been able to sleep. Lately, you are the main focus of my prayers. Please tell me what in all that makes ME your enemy!"

She explained nothing, simply flung her head, rolled her eyes, and stormed away. Even though I hadn't a clue of what I could have done that was so awful, I felt terrible. It was obvious that Lyn believed I had done something. Therefore, I was·determined to get to the bottom of her complaint.

After just standing in the hall for about five minutes, trying to figure Lynzi out, the first period bell rung. Being that I was on the other side of the building, I took off running. I guess it wasn't my day because as soon as I turned the corner, I bumped straight into Dr. Franklin.

He jokingly laughed, "Ah, Miss Skky, I wasn't informed that the track team tryouts were being held this morning . . . in the school!"

"Doc, I'm sorry," I gasped practically out of breath. "I'll slow it down."

"Slow it down? Oh no, I don't think so. You'd better retreat to walking. Now, I am going to let you slide this time. Do not let me catch you running again, ya hear?"

"Yes sir," I answered with a smile, as he wrote me a pass to my class.

The tardy bell rung just as I bumped into the principal. Luckily, he was in a good mood. Usually, though, he looks out for me.

It seemed like déjà vu when I saw Dymond. She too didn't want anything to do with me. Her rationale was just as vague as Lynzi's. Is this a conspiracy, or did I bump my head and not remember what awful deeds I had done to my girls?

I said, "Hey girl, what's goin' on?"

Dymond snarled, "Talk to the hand, baby 'cause the ears ain't listening. We have nothin' to say to one another."

"Are you mad?" I asked as if I couldn't read her stand-offish actions.

"You know, Pay, I don't even have the time," Dy paused, huffed, and said, "or the energy to deal with you. You've really irked me!"

She then threw her hand in my face. I was livid. I started to snatch her arm and yank the heck out of it. I mean, it's one thing to be mad at me, but it's another to disrespect me.

After class was over, it was my mission to find Rain. Just needed a friend, I guess. Hoped she wasn't mad as well. Walking out the door, Dymond bumped into me. That's when I kinda lost it. I had had enough of the nonsense.

I growled, "Dy, I don't know what your problem is. I haven't done a thang to ya. So, why are you acting all crazy? Be real. Tell me, what's up with the attitude?"

"I can't believe you're playing innocent," she abruptly turned and said. "I tell you every piece of information I ever get. Dymond knows . . . Payton knows. But you, no, you don't trust me enough to return the same courtesy. Girl, I thought you was my girrrl. Huh, now I see it was just a one-way street. I don't have the patience or the time to drive down that road."

Oh, was she making me mad. She didn't give me a chance to respond. Dymond took off to her next class, with her nose held high. Obviously, our friendship meant nothing.

In the five minutes we had between classes, I was more determined than before to track Rain down. Maybe she could fill in the missing pieces, which Lyn and Dy wrongfully assumed I already knew. While scurrying to locate her, I prayed for our confrontation. I didn't need her to freak out too.

"Rain," I shouted as I spotted her dashing from one side of Laney High to the other. "Stop, stop—it's me, Pay!"

As soon as she saw me, Rain flew my way. She shook her head. Right then and there, I realized something was up. But what? I thought.

"Chile," she gasped, "I've been looking for you all morning. Girl, our girls had it out this morning. Worse, both of them are mad at you. But, you probably know that part by now, huh?"

I said with anger, "Yeah, I know they're upset. But I haven't done anything to either one of them. I'm clueless as to what this latest mess is all about. They were both vague with me. Tell me what's going on, please."

"I can't talk about it now. It's too long. I'll hip you to it after school," Rain voiced as if she was in a huge hurry.

I blurted out, "No, no, don't trip. You can't leave me hangin.'"

"OK," Rain began, "here it is on the quick tip. I'll go into more details later. This morning Dy cornered Lyn and went off. You know how Dymond likes to know . . . everything. Well, she told Lynzi that she couldn't believe Lynzi didn't tell her about her situation. You know, the fact that she's pregnant and all. Of course, Lynzi was upset that she knew. Dy was hot that she didn't know. So, they exchanged a few harsh words and Dymond stormed away. Before I could get a word in, Lynzi shouted that she was furious with you."

"Why didn't you say something after that?" I questioned.

Rain spoke up, "I tried! Believe me, I tried. As soon as I opened my mouth, though, Lyn walked away. She told me she didn't want to hear me taking up for you. But listen, this will get straightened out. I got to get to class. We'll talk."

Well, at least I finally had a clear understanding of what was going on. Yep, now I got it. Lynzi's upset with me 'cause she thinks I told Dymond and Rain what's going on with her. Miss Dy is disturbed because I didn't tell her someone else's business. How twisted!

Surely all this mess could be put in check quickly when I spoke to them about their prospective beefs with me. So, I didn't sweat it the rest of the day. If they wanna act all crazy about stuff I did not do and could not do, then that's on them.

The week surely didn't fly by this time. This was the longest Monday through Friday I'd had in a while. You would have thought I had the plague, the way everyone stayed away.

Believe me, I tried to straighten things out with my friends. But their anger towards me turned to rage. Rain and I were still cool; however, even she was a bit distant this week.

I couldn't walk down a hall without hearing people whisper 'bout me and my crew. Misinformation, lies, and gossip were what they were spreading. And when they noticed that I could hear them, they gave fake smiles and turned away.

I prayed, "Lord, I try so hard to live right. Sure, I fall short a lot. I even admit that I don't always think the purest thoughts. This situation, though, seems so cruel and unfair. Two people that I care about hate me. What's up with this? Should I just forget them and press on? Is that what You're trying to tell me? It says in Romans 8:28, 'All things work together for the good.' Well, I can't dispute what it says, but ever since Lynzi came to me with this whole pregnancy thang, I've had one headache after another. Now, tell me, how could that possibly be good? Father, do You hear my sorrow? Help if You do, please!"

——————————

"What is she doing here?" Dymond uttered in a rude voice. We were sitting in Rain's house, at her invitation. Neither of us knew the other would be there.

"You know what? I don't know what's going on here, but I did not come here to be harassed, Rain," I voiced, basically tired of it all.

Rain spoke out, "No, no, no. Don't get upset or ask questions ya'll. Just bear with me and—"

The doorbell rang and interrupted her thoughts. I think both Dy and I had a clear idea of who it was. Rain left the two of us sitting alone. It felt like I was the only one there. We said nothing. We looked everywhere but at one another. Sadly, this same cold person had been my friend a week ago.

When Rain came back to the den, she wasn't alone. Yep, I had a feeling it was Lynzi. I didn't even look up; the fact was confirmed when her annoying voice irritated my eardrums.

"I don't EVEN think so," Lynzi yelled at the top of her voice.

Rain grabbed Lynzi as she tried to walk away and said, "Just sit down. Sit right down."

Wow, I thought, *here it was I assumed that Rain could care less.* How wrong I was. She was trying desperately to get us all back together. I should have known I could count on her. Even if her ploy proves to be unsuccessful, I'll never sway from trusting her motives again.

"I invited you all to sleep over because there's a few things that I want to say," Rain started as she huffed with nervousness.

"When I agreed to come," Dy lashed out, "I was under the impression that my presence was the only one you needed to keep you company!"

I blurted, "In other words, she didn't know I'd be here."

"Believe me," Lynzi interjected, "I wouldn't have come if I'd known you would be here either."

Rain, like an ambulance, came to my rescue when she said, "Come on guys. All this is ridiculous. Payton is being totally misunderstood here."

"Chile, you just taking up fer her 'cause she yo best friend. Please, I don't wanna hear it," Dymond announced with her arms crossed and her head tilted.

Lynzi agreed, "Uh-huh, that's right. It's easy for you to say, when she did not tell any of your business."

At that point, I might as well have been a pot of water on the stove turned too high. I was boiling! I was so hot that sweat balls were falling from my head to the floor. All week I had been trying to convince myself that I did not care what Lynzi or Dymond thought of me. With the way my body was reacting, I guess that theory stopped cooking.

"Did you ever ask Payton if she told?" Rain asked Lynzi.

Lynzi responded slowly, "I—I didn't need to ask. Dannng, she didn't deny the fact."

"You never gave me a chance!" I said in a mean way.

Lynzi asked, almost dumbfounded, "What—what do you mean?"

"I'll explain," Rain cut in.

I had no clue what Rain was going to say. A look of confusion was on my face, not knowing what was about to come out. Shucks, I didn't even know myself how this information got leaked. Seemed everyone in the whole darn school knew. If I were Lyn, I probably would have thought she spread my business too.

That's the thing; I never said a word to anyone. I've racked my brain to figure who told. No one else knew!

Rain said, "Well, I was trying to determine how this all happened. 'Cause if Payton told me she didn't say anything, then I know she didn't say anything. Now I admit, at first I was a little mad that she didn't tell me what she knew. But you, Dy, you were livid. And Lyn, as mad as you were at Payton, I knew you silenced her to secrecy. So, I couldn't be mad at that. Dymond, you shouldn't be angry that she didn't tell you either."

"You mean you didn't tell . . . anybody?" Lynzi questioned in disbelief.

I looked her eye-to-eye and said, "No! I never betrayed you. I have been trying to tell you that all week, but you've been blowing me off."

"Well then . . . who told?" Lynzi uttered, practically ashamed that she accused the wrong person.

Rain told us that yesterday she'd seen Bam in the hall. They overheard some busybodies talking about the whole thing. Bam told Rain he didn't mean for this to blow up like it did. Then he slipped and said, as he banged on the lockers, that he should not have told Dakari.

Well, right when Rain breathed the word Dakari, I knew what had happened. Dakari told Fatz and Fatz told everyone else, especially Dymond. Dy in anger told Rain. Yep, that's how it spread, as easily as butter on a toasted piece of bread.

Rain said, "So, Lynzi, it was never Payton that spilled the beans. It was Bam! The love you're back together with actually let you down. Surprise, surprise!"

I couldn't believe I didn't think of Bam myself. Shoot, other than me, he was the only one who knew. Why in the world would he divulge his own business like that. And then Dakari . . . Guess I'm not the only one Dakari is letting down these days.

The next few minutes were full of apologies. Lynzi was kind enough to clear me with Dy. She explained everything. Lynzi told them that she had planned to tell them, but she was ashamed. They were cool with her reasoning. Finally, the four of us were laughing again. In their "I'm sorries," they said it was their mission to get me a date for the cotillion.

Life was good again. Well, except Lynzi's problem still existed. We ordered pizza, watched movies, and chatted away. Felt like it had been so long since we'd hung out.

The four of us cried. We laughed. We sang out of key to music videos. And we joked.

Then we finally broke into the unsafe place, Lynzi's problem. None of us wanted to go there. However, we all knew we had to.

So, I asked the tough question. "Girl, have you gone to the doctor?"

"OK, don't ya'll get on me. I'm gonna go. I'll go tomorrow. Yeah, tomorrow's Saturday. I'll go then. You know . . . why don't all you guys come with me? Please, I need your support more than ever. Planned Parenthood is where we'll go. I just . . . don't know what I'm gonna do," Lynzi cried as tears trickled down her face like it was a stream.

Each of us reaffirmed good things to her. We told her that we'd be there and that things would be OK. Her pain was ours.

The lights were off and in the darkness I thought, *A slumber party has never meant so much to me before.* I had to let them know.

I whispered with a slight crackle in my voice, "You guys awake? Listen . . . I care so much about each of you. This was one of the worst weeks of my life. Losing your friendships felt just as bad as losing big-head Dakari. Every time I kept thinking we would not be this tight again, the pain got worse. I count on you guys to be there. I love ya'll!"

They said in unison, "We love you too!"

The next morning was pretty scary for all of us. Lynzi was on her way to confirm her pregnancy. We were all very quiet, kinda solemn, not knowing what the next step would be. However, we couldn't get there till this was taken care of. The doctor had to at least tell her how far along she was, and make sure both she and the baby were OK.

Of course, Lynzi's main reason for going was to find out all about abortion. Dymond seconded that. Rain and I tried over and over to tell her that wasn't the way to go. We were split, yet unified.

When we got to the front of the place, we stared at the building twenty feet away. PLANNED PARENTHOOD! Those two words seemed ridiculous. First of all, nothing about this situation was planned. Lynzi definitely didn't need to be a parent. If she did have a kid, she'd be struggling to stay out of the 'hood. 'Cause she won't have a job.

"Well, no need to wait. Let's go," I informed.

Lynzi grunted, "I'm—I'm scared."

"Lynzi." Rain spoke to comfort her, "We're here with you."

"Girrrl, come on, you gotta do it sometime," Dy announced. "The quicker you go in the faster you can get out!"

Lynzi stalled, "Can we just pray? I need some prayer. Pay, why don't you lead?"

Agreeing with her idea, I voiced, "That's fine. Let's all pray."

Since I drove and Rain was in the front passenger seat, we turned around. All four of us held hands. The grip was so tight.

"OK," I began, "I'll dial and Lynzi, then you go. Dy, you pray after her, and Rain, you hang up. Father, thank You so much for loving us. We realize that it is only Your grace which allowed us to get back together as friends. All of us are frightened right now. We need Your protection. Please give my friend peace as she talks to this doctor. Help her make the right decision. I've asked You for a miracle so many times before, but now I'm asking again."

I ended and squeezed Lynzi's hand, then she began, "God, I'm so . . . just . . . so . . . help me! I don't want to let You down ever again. God, I can't . . . can't raise a baby. I need . . ."

"Lord, I'm a lil' shaken up too," Dymond continued, because obviously as upset as Lynzi was, she could not go on. "I admit things are not really the way they're suppose to be and stuff. I mean, You gotta help a sista out. Be on our side and all. Make things right, like only You can."

Dy squeezed and Rain said, "Dearest Master, we praise You right now because You are so awesome. And although this situation looks bleak, I have faith, Lord, that You're gonna do great things in the midst of turmoil. You are gonna blow our minds with Your next move. Yea though we walk through the darkness, we can keep treading, for we are walking with You. Amen!"

We had been sitting in the waiting room for sixteen minutes, anticipating the big moment that a nurse would escort Lynzi back to be examined. The place seemed so cold! So definite! So final!

I had no clue what each of them were thinking. My thoughts were riveting and frigid. I may not have been able to read their minds, but we were all as one, holding hands in as strong a grip as you'd ever get.

"Lynzi?" the tall blonde nurse called.

"That's me . . . unfortunately," Lynzi hesitantly stated.

Rain looked at me and asked, "Why didn't they call her last name too?"

"I think here at Planned Parenthood," I hoped to correctly explain, "it's like an anonymous thang. Suppose to be a safe place for girls to go and receive correct information.

121

I'm not one hundred percent sure though."

The next thirty minutes were intense. All types of bad thoughts were swimming around in my brain. Among the three of us, we read every piece of literature in the place, from herpes to AIDS, from condoms to diaphragms, and from breast cancer to cancer of the cervix. If we ever needed a reason why God is against premarital sex, that day we found tons of reasons why we should abstain.

"I don't know what Lynzi is gonna do with a child," Rain expressed to Dy and me, almost breaking down.

We shook our heads to agree. Before we could say another word, we heard Lynzi screaming. We were even more scared now.

"I'M NOT PREGNANT! I'M NOT HAVING A KID! YES," she yelled with tears of joy.

Of course, we had lots of questions. So, she explained. Basically, when her test at the doctor's office came back negative, she was beside herself. Lynzi then told the nurse that three tests at home had come back positive. Therefore, they retested her, this time drawing blood. When that test came back negative too, she pulled one of her home test indicators from her purse.

The nurse laughed, after she examined it thoroughly. Can you believe it was an ovulation predictor kit, not a pregnancy test? With abnormal cycles, Lynzi was ovulating when she took the test. Not pregnant! Her period should be on any day. Lyn told us that she remembers quickly getting the box at the drug store 'cause she saw some of our classmates getting personal items.

All the way home we rejoiced. God is good! Everyone except Dymond vowed to leave sex alone. Dy said she'd try, but realistically, she'd just have to agree to be careful.

God proved once again that He knows what's best. Luckily, we won't have to face the tough choice. You better believe we will not forget this lesson. We thought that we were just passing the time, but the heavenly Father was testing our faith—and testing our friendship.

10

Ringing My Heart

inally, the holidays! It was around forty degrees. So many changes in Augusta this time of year. The smell of barbecue and the sight of fireworks were no longer present in the air. Last-minute Christmas shoppers bustled back and forth. And me, well, my mind was filled with thoughts of Joseph, Mary, and baby Jesus, the true reason for the season.

Finals were the toughest they'd ever been. Probably all those honor classes. I think I did pretty good, though. Shucks, I sure studied enough. My social life had gone out the window the past few weeks. So, I was really looking forward to this break.

Get to hang tough with my girls. Well, that is, after my family gets back from Conyers, Georgia. That's where my paternal grandparents live. It's about two hours away. Tradition, yep tradition, dictates that I'm there Christmas Eve and Christmas morn.

"Hun—nee," my seventy-two-year-old grandma said, "phone fer ya. Bay—bee, get on up na, ya here. Get on up out that they bed and get it."

Who in the world would be tracking me in Conyers? I glanced at the time, while wiping the cornbread sleep from the corner of my eye. The clock read five thirty A.M. Now, I was hot!

"OK, who's got the nerve to disturb my entire family on Christmas morning?" I asked after bumping into two doors trying to answer the phone.

"Merry Christmas to ya, Merry Christmas to ya, Merrrry Christ—mas!" the out-of-key chorus comprised of my three best friends sang.

I said kinda laughing, "Oh, you guys are crazy! Aren't ya'll a tad bit too old to be staying up all night waiting for Santa?"

"Ha, ha, ha," Lynzi uttered sarcastically, "we all just woke up. Wanted to wish you a merry holiday and all. Shoot, a sista can't even appreciate when folks try and do somethin' nice."

"Girrrl," I chuckled, "don't even try it. What ya'll really want? Waking my grandma up . . ."

Dymond boldly stated, "Chile, please, you know Grandma Wilva Mae been up since the crack of dawn, fixin' her younguns some grits and bacon."

"It ain't the crack of dawn yet," I told them.

"Cool," Dymond replied, "then she won't need her alarm clock. Consider us her wake-up call."

We all laughed. They knew my family so well. I could smell the scrumptious buttermilk biscuits baking in the oven. Equally, I knew them just as well. Although it was kinda special hearing from them all, I felt there was much more behind the dime.

"Now I'm asking again. Tell me what's really up." I questioned for the second time.

"Well," Rain hesitated, "don't get us wrong; we want you to have a most joyous holiday in Conyers. But, are you coming back in time enough to drive us to the area basketball tournament? Remember, the semi-finals start tonight. Tyson's playing and you gotta cheer."

"OK, I'll swoop ya'll," I responded without hesitation.

The place was packed! Tonight and tomorrow folks will be here from everywhere. Last week sixteen high schools entered. Twelve were eliminated and four are still shootin' strong. Laney, my school, T. W. Josey, Tyson's team, Silver Bluff from Aiken, and Jackson High.

Our team played Silver Bluff first. Lynzi and I were in the girls' locker room warming up. The rest of the squad were already on the court. Hanging with Lynzi always seemed to make me lag behind.

Just as the two of us were finally headed to cheer, Dymond and Rain burst in. They were giggling like two little kindergartners who just stole a cookie from the cookie jar. At last, they calmed down enough to explain what was going on.

"Boy, do we have a surprise for you," Dymond said smilingly from ear to ear, as she stared at me.

"What do you mean, a surprise?" I questioned, hoping that they weren't about to play a practical joke.

"Come on," Rain uttered as she pulled me on one hand and Dy yanked the other arm.

As soon as we stepped out on the court, they pointed my head in the direction of a Silver Bluff guard. He was wearing number forty. His back was to me. I admit, his build was pretty nice and all, but what was the big deal?

When he turned toward me to shoot a jumper, I was floored. Of all people, surprise, surprise. It was Tad Taylor. *No way,* I thought with pleasure. I knew he was from Aiken, but I didn't know he went to Silver Bluff. My thoughts were changing every second. Ironically, though, they were all thoughts of him.

Now, it was the second half of the game. My eyes had not detoured from him. We were losing, yet I was glad. Deep down, I found myself cheering for his school instead of Laney.

He ran up and down the court like the lead race car in a derby; swift, powerful, and in charge. Such charisma and ease. Boy, was I impressed. Most of me wanted to run right on the court and hug him. But I thought about it, and really I didn't even know this guy.

He was supposed to call. Actually, with everything I had going on, until this moment I had forgotten all about him anyway. Maybe he's got a girl now. Wouldn't that be just my luck?

Tad was so good with the basketball, it almost slipped my mind that he was great at football too. He was makin' some bad moves. He shot three-pointers like he was standing right under the basket. The ball just tipped in. It seemed effortless.

"Well, we're out of the tournament," Lynzi stated as the buzzer sounded and the scoreboard read Laney 55, Silver Bluff 76.

Dymond, Rain, Lynzi, and I were huddled up watching the next game. Rain screamed for Tyson so loud it became embarrassing. He could ball, though. I gotta give 'im his props. He had twenty-five points and it was just the first half. Folks called him "Air Tyson"!

"Where you guys goin'?" I said to the three of them as they got up to leave me.

Dymond announced, "It's halftime. Ain't nobody gonna sit here all night. We gon' make some rounds. Us important folks got people to see. You can sit here if ya want to. Check ya on the rebound."

"Come go with us," Lynzi invited. "We'll be back before the second half."

I quickly replied, "No thanks! I'm tired from cheering. Plus, with all these people crowded in here, it will be the fourth quarter before you get to the concession stand."

You know, sometimes we just act crazy. To the left of me were two sistas cursing each other out. On the top bleacher a couple was practically having sex. These dudes straight across were smokin' weed. You'd think I was at a club instead of a basketball game. All of a sudden, some unknown pervert grabbed my neck and kissed it before I could stop him. This jerk I had never seen before was about five-feet one inch. The shrimp's breath reeked of alcohol.

"Let me go!" I demanded forcefully.

"Why you tryin' to play me, sista? Ya know you like this," he barely gasped with his bloodshot, red eyes.

"Take your filthy paws off me," I screamed. "Take them off!"

He said all cool, "Ah, don't try to act all proper on a nig . . ."

"Please," I pleaded, "LEAVE ME ALONE!"

"Come on," he sobbed, just as he tried desperately to fondle me.

I pushed him to stop his actions. In anger, he threw up his fist to punch me. I was terrified. It was a blessing when someone grabbed his arm.

"Get off the lady. Hit me if you want to hit somebody," the nice guy said.

"Naw man, I don't want no trouble. I'm—I'm outta here," the dog replied like the coward I knew he was.

My gosh, was I shaken up! So much so that I couldn't even look up to thank my hero. My head was bowed down and my eyes were filling with tears.

"I've got to get out of here," I whispered to myself.

This guy uttered with deep concern, "Are you OK?"

When I finally looked into his kind eyes, I felt like Cinderella. There was Tad Taylor standing before me. My Prince Charming! It had to be an angel that brought us together this way.

"Come on, I'll get you out of here the back way," he said to me. "You need some air, and I don't think it's wise for you to be alone."

Before I could respond, he grabbed my hand and whisked me away. At that point, I had forgotten all about the rude dude. Tad had found me. Oh, how sweet! I still couldn't believe he stepped in the middle of my confrontation. That crazy boy might have had a gun, knife, gang, anything.

When we got outside, he pulled a Coke from his bag and said, "Here, drink this."

I took it graciously and said, "Tad, I can't thank you enough. That was so sweet of you to help me like that. I mean, how'd you see me? How did you know I needed help?"

"I was in the hall 'bout to break outta here, when I ran into your girls. Of course, they wouldn't let me go until they pointed you out. But . . . I was kinda glad. I've been crazy busy with all going on that I haven't had a chance to give you a ring. I have wanted to call, though."

He wanted to call. Oh yes! I was starting to feel something here.

Tad continued, "After your friends told me where you were sitting, I figured I should at least come and speak. As I found my way over to ya, I saw the boy disrespecting you. He was getting louder and his hands were in the wrong place. I didn't do nothing special. I did what any gentleman would do. It wasn't a big deal. I'm only glad I could help. Besides, you'd do the same thing for me, wouldn't you?"

We both laughed. I loved his sense of humility. His

sense of humor was an added plus.

"So, are you about to leave?" I asked hoping he'd say no.

"I got a little time," he told me in a cute, fun way.

The two of us walked around the school. The place was unfamiliar to us both, since neither of us attended there. We walked, not saying anything, but smiling from time to time.

Tad wasn't holding my hand anymore. Guess there's no reason he should. He only did that in the first place to lead me outside safely. Once he did that, he let it go. But boy, did I want to grab his. Stroke his hand! Caress his fingers! Memorize his fingerprint!

We finally stopped walking when we reached the front of the school. We sat on a bench. The temperature was steadily dropping around us. Yet, I felt my heart warming up. And why? Guess the mystic was boiling me over.

"So, Miss Payton Skky, tell me a little bit about you," Tad asked with interest.

"You wanna know about me?" I uttered trying to charm him. "There's really not much to tell. Honestly, I'm rather boring. I do stuff with the school. Have an annoying brother. Wonderful folks, most of the time. Cool friends, in the 'in crowd.' Nothing spectacular. What about you? You're the MAN! The man who just threw down in there. Actually, I'm surprised you aren't riding with your team."

"Usually I do have to. Coach let us slide this time, since it's Christmas. Umm . . . about me. Well, I live in South Carolina. You know that. More than anything, I am proud to say that I'm a Christian. That fact makes today awful special, being that it is Jesus Christ's birthday. Ever since the day I gave my life to Him, which was about three years ago, things have been the bomb. Every day I surrender to His will. More and more, I'm amazed at what He does through me. Like the game tonight. Totally the Lord," Tad spoke in awe as he looked towards heaven.

What a deep brother. I love Jesus, too, but I don't ever

130

really discuss Him with others. So, I stared at the sky with Tad. All the stars were so breathtaking. One was shining amazingly bright. Seemed as if it was a sign from that angel, OKing our being together. Crazy, huh?

I inquired, "What do you think of when you see that star?"

"I think of Bethlehem! Think if I follow it, it will lead me to where Jesus was born. I think of the creep who just tried to fondle you. He's so far removed from respecting what today is, till it is sad. The brother has no clue who's really in charge. Just living for today. Living for himself. That star reminds me who we all need to be living for," he stated with passion and conviction.

What a guy. He's so different from most boys I know. Here he was MVP of a game and he takes the focus off himself.

Tad kept talking. "Hey, I hope I'm not losing you or boring you. Just tryin' to keep it real and tell you what I'm about. A lot of people nowadays can't deal with that. So, I've been praying to God for a friend. Not a girlfriend. Not a home boy. But a true friend. With all my success in football, people have constantly been there. God has given me a spirit of discernment. He's been showing me that quite a few of the people I hang tough with don't mean me no good. I don't mind rollin' by myself, but it'd be cool—real cool—to be with someone who sincerely cared about Tad. I'm straight tired of fake folks being down with the bandwagon. Shoooot, the wagon could stop any day."

We talked, and talked, and talked, and talked. Then we talked some more. What was neat is that I enjoyed every word he breathed. Before we knew it, people were coming out of the gym.

"I gotta get to my car. My friends are probably looking for me. I drove," I said reluctantly. "You have my number. Feel free to use it."

"I'll just walk you around the corner, until we see your car. Don't want any more trouble. Tomorrow I have to play in the final game. I hope you come and cheer me on this time," Tad said, blushing.

Without answering, I smiled because, little did he know, I cheered for him tonight. We said quick goodbyes and I jetted to my jeep. The ride home was hilarious. A bunch of noisy busybodies. Rain probed me to see if I liked Tad. Lynzi quizzed me about whether he was going to be my date at the cotillion. And Dy interrogated me to find out if I kissed him.

I brushed them all off. Had to play down the talk Tad and I shared. After all, I still hadn't figured this guy out. Didn't know what type of relationship he wanted with me. He mentioned praying for a friend. But what does that really mean? Until I know that, I can't answer any of their questions.

"So who won the last game?" I asked.

Rain proudly replied, "You know my baby carried T. W. Josey to a victory. My beau . . . will play your beau . . . for the title."

"My beau?" I gasped. "It's not even like that. He's a nice guy—a really nice guy. Who knows what will happen, if anything?"

For the sake of possible embarrassment, I was telling them one thing. However, deep down I was truly hoping Tad and I would turn into something as wonderful as that beautiful shining star, still draped perfectly in the dark blue sky. Guys with values are rare. Gotta hold on if you're ever lucky enough to find one. I wish I knew what Tad wanted for us, if anything.

New Year's Eve was here. One year down, another one upon us. My parents didn't want me out in the streets. The debs were having a party, but this was the one and only

132

event my mother felt was too dangerous for me to attend. So, to feel like I wasn't imprisoned, they allowed me to have the girls over.

We had a crab feast. Four dozen steamed whole crabs, all piled on the kitchen table. We called it our way to claw into what's to come.

Later, we were all swarmed around the fireplace, trying to sing carols, even though Christmas was last week. Then they asked the question I was dreading.

"What's up? You talked to O'boy?" Dymond said inquisitively.

"Ah, look at her," Rain stated with a smile. "She's trying to keep it to herself. Don't pressure her."

Lynzi threw in her two cents with, "Bump that! Tell us somethin.'"

I was about to break down. Just cry, right then and there. Wanted to scream at the top of my lungs.

But I got a hold of my emotions and said, "He hasn't called. It's been a whole week and he hasn't dialed my number once. So, can we please talk about something else?"

The live countdown from New York was on TV. We were half tuned in to it and partly into thumbing through magazines. My folks were upstairs playing spades with my godparents.

It was now fifteen minutes till the New Year. Rain and I went to the kitchen to get the champagne glasses out of the freezer and the sparkling cider from the fridge. Toasting to our dreams would be the highlight of the night. As the two of us headed downstairs, my dad stopped us.

"Payton dear," he uttered while showing me his trump tight hand, "is that your phone I hear ringing this time of night? Don't be on long."

I wondered which one of my friends' beaus was calling. Was it Fatz for Dy, Tyson for Rain, or Bam for Lynzi? Whoever, it was not for me. As I strolled to my room to pick

133

it up, the answering machine came on.

I was trying to grab it when the guy said, "Hello, Payton, this is—"

"I know who this is," I grabbed the phone and blurted out in a surprised yet happy tone.

"Oh, so you're screening your calls?" he asked.

"No, Tad," I answered. "The machine just picked up before I got to it."

"Well, I hope I'm not calling too late. Since it is midnight, I won't keep you too long. First of all, I want to apologize for not getting a chance to call you this week. I'm sure you don't want to hear excuses. But, I will say a lot has been going on. I have been thinking about you. Truly enjoyed our conversation the other night. I find you to be a pretty interesting lady. I didn't know what you had up tonight. But I'm glad I caught you. See, I hoped to be the last person you spoke with this year and the first person you talked with next," Tad mumbled, sounding sincere.

I was stunned. It felt like a muzzle was placed on my mouth. Were my ears hearing him correctly?

I gained composure and knew I couldn't get too excited. Not trying to go on another roller coaster ride. Just a week ago, I got all pumped to chat with him and he didn't even call. Won't let myself get up like that again. Too far of a drop if he lets me down.

"Tad, my friends are downstairs. I'd love to extend this conversation, but now is not a good time," I said coldly.

"Ah, I see you're mad at me, huh?" Tad asked with a smirk in his tone.

I asked, "Why—why would you say that?"

"Look, let's cut through the ice. I apologize for not calling when I said I would. Either way you've gotta believe I meant to. I went back over to the University of Georgia. February is when I'm supposed to declare what school I want to attend. Only trying to make good decisions. So,

134

since school's out, I took advantage of the time off to again visit my first choice. You know, I could explain and explain, but I'm sure you don't wanna hear the boring details. You said you need to go, so I'll let you. It was my mistake for calling. Bye, Payton," Tad voiced as he was about to hang up.

"No. No, wait! Maybe I was a little harsh," I quickly uttered, hoping to keep him on the line. "I've got a few seconds."

"OK," Tad replied, "Tell me, Miss Skky, what was the greatest thing that happened to you this year?"

"For me, it was learning how important it is to have faith in God. Even when things seem a little crazy and the boat starts rocking on the stormy water, I found that if you stay with Him, the boat will stop rocking and you'll make it to the shore of peace," I told him.

Tad said, "That's exciting! I've never heard you talk of God like that. What do you expect from next year?"

"Whatever, the Lord gives, I will take," I responded with humility.

Talking to him was such a joy for me. I realized an even greater prize. That treasure is how much I'd grown in my walk with Christ. Uttering those words to him as to what I expect out of next year allowed me to realize my priorities were in the right order.

"You're quiet! Did you hear me? Happy New Year, Payton," Tad responded.

"Wow!" I blabbed. "It's here already! Happy New Year to you, Mr. Taylor."

He said, "I know you've got company, so I won't hold you. But I want to ask if you'd like to go to a movie later today?"

"Tonight's good," I said, unaware his invitation was coming.

"Then I'll phone you back later with details," Tad replied. "Enjoy your friends and tell them hello!"

When we ended the conversation, I was ecstatic. Tad

called. Yes!

Before I could exit my room, Dy, Rain, and Lynzi invaded. They were laughing, smiling, and cutting up. Basically, I knew then that they had eavesdropped. They pretty much heard the entire thing.

After they realized that I knew they knew it was Tad, we all screamed with excitement! Then we hugged each other. Such a special moment.

"Come on ya'll, enough of the sentimental stuff. We've got to get downstairs and bring in the New Year right. Our toast—remember," Rain yelled trying to sway us to the basement.

I glanced at them all, dived backwards on my bed, and shouted, "Who can concentrate on bringing in the New Year when I'm all shaken up with the way Tad Taylor is ringing my heart!"

11

Falling for Chocolate

"Thanks, but no thanks. I don't like chocolate," I said to Tad as he offered me his M&Ms.

"What? You don't like chocolate? That's my nickname. My whole family calls me chocolate. Plus, I love any dish with chocolate in it. What's your problem with it?" he asked. "Don't you just love chocolate malts, chocolate syrup heated and draped over a brownie, and chocolate chip cookies? Ooh, you're missing out. Hang with me though; you'll learn to like chocolate a whole lot."

I giggled, "Tad you're so silly!"

The two of us had really been enjoying one another. Spending so much time together. We were working on an awesome friendship.

He's such a gentleman. I had learned quite a bit about him. He was transparent. I liked that. No surprises. Only truth!

The movies, the restaurants, the mall, the bowling alley, the skating rink, the city park, the billiard hall, and more—

name it, we tried it. Our dates were filled with so much. We did it all and we liked doing it together.

It was now three weeks into the New Year and we had talked every day. So, now it was time for the next step. Getting to know parents. We were both a bit apprehensive. But, I had confidence that it would go well. At least, I hoped it would.

My side was first. Tad was invited over for Sunday dinner. My parents had briefly met him when he picked me up for an outing. They just didn't know the brother. If you get my meaning.

My dad said to my brother, "Who is this guy? You ever heard of him, Perry?"

"I haven't met him, Pops, but he's supposed to be pretty cool. I know he's the top football recruit in the state of South Carolina. All the SEC schools want him to play for their team. The word is out that he really digs Payton. So, ya know I'm gon' drill him," my brother replied.

"No, son," my father commented, "we are going to drill him."

I dashed into the room they were in and said, "Hey, there will be none of that drilling stuff. Tad is a very nice guy. I assure you, Daddy, there's nothing not to like about him. Please, please don't give him a hard time."

My mother summoned me back into the kitchen. She handed me the china to set the table. Such an elegant dinner she had prepared! My mother is the ultimate hostess.

I was praying that Tad knew table etiquette. The one thing that would frustrate my mother would be if he didn't know which fork to use. If that happened, she definitely would not want him to be my date for the ball.

Finally, he arrived. He was exactly on time. Not a minute early and not a minute late. My mother smiled when

138

she noticed the clock. I realized then, Tad had begun racking up positive points with her.

I wanted so bad to answer the door. Of course, Mommy Dearest held me back. She suggested that it wasn't a lady's place to look and act anxious.

Perry got it and said, "Come on in, man."

"Son, who's that at the door?" my dad blurted out.

"Ah, Dad, come on," Perry said jokingly, knowing my father was about to give Tad a hard time.

"Is that the tackhead joker Payton's been carrying on about? Well, tell him he can't come in. There aren't any free meals here. Just kidding! Come on up," my dad invited from the living room.

Tad came up and shook my dad's hand. Three of them dived straight into the topic of football. Of course, that eased Tad. My father loved gabbing about sports, with his "back in the day" stories. Perry, being a sophomore, was taking mental notes. So far it seemed to be going pretty well.

After helping my mother in the kitchen, my family went to freshen up. That left Tad and I alone. I gave him a huge hug. His suave appearance was stunning.

"So, are you nervous?" I questioned. He answered, "A tad!"

We laughed and I said, "Seriously though, I'm really glad you're here. And whatever my family says, please don't hold it against me."

"I could hold nothing against you. You are too precious," he smiled and said.

Dinner was full of chatter. But then I noticed everyone was running their mouth except Tad. He appeared shaken, scared, nervous, and confused all rolled into one. He was seated to the right of my father.

I know he desired to be impressive and acceptable to my family. In his haste to be splendid at the table, he made a wrong move. Can you believe he drank from the wrong tea glass? I guess his head and his hands were not in sync 'cause they acted independently. Somehow he sipped my father's cup.

Yes, it was embarrassing. Tad apologized again and again. But even my dad fessed up to the fact it is difficult for anyone to maintain their composure in that situation.

We took a break from each other the next five days. I think it was our way of trying to slow things down. Frankly, I have no clue why I agreed to it. I loved that the ball was rolling. However, when Tad suggested it, I didn't want him to know I was head over heels. Therefore, I quickly agreed; time off would be fine.

Tad wasn't my boyfriend; nevertheless, I was beginning to feel attached. Being in school without him makes a girl's mind wander. I know how popular Dakari is at Laney. Even though Mr. Graham is spoken for, girls are still crazy about him. He turns heads in the halls every day.

I can only imagine that Tad has it the same way at Silver Bluff. Oh no, what if he wanted to take time out because he wanted to try a girl at his school? Naw, surely if they had anybody worth keeping his attention, his eye would have never peeped over at me.

Finally, it was Friday night. He hadn't called. I wanted so desperately to just pick up the phone already. Unfortunately, he had always pursued me. Didn't wanna break that pattern.

It was getting late. Even though I was tempted to phone him, it would be rude to his family. Observing Rain's tough situation with Tyson's mother allowed me to clearly understand that I didn't want to give Tad's parents any reason to dislike me. So, I forced myself to go to sleep. I tossed and turned, turned and tossed. At last I relaxed as I thought of the past few weeks. Those sweet memories turned into an extended dream.

The next thing I knew it was morning. I was awakened, not by my mother's screaming voice telling me to get out of bed and do my chores, but by a call.

"Payton, it's me, Tad," he said.

With a raspy voice, I replied, "Tad . . . how've you been?"

"I've been OK. I admit, this week has been a little dull since you haven't been in it. I missed you. Know it's last minute and everything, but I was hoping we could get together today?" he asked.

"Umm . . . I have to do some stuff for my mom. The usual Saturday duties await me. If I get in it, I should be done around noon. What did you have in mind?" I questioned.

He answered, "I'd like to invite you out my way. My folks would like to meet the girl I've been bragging about. I promise it will be painless. Plus, I got a fun surprise planned."

"I'll run it by my mother. I don't think it'll be a problem," I said to him. "What should I wear?"

"Nothing fancy . . . jeans and a coat," he uttered.

From the time I hung up the phone to the moment he arrived to pick me up, the minutes passed too slow. I was so glad to see him. It felt as if it had been ages since we were together.

Hugs, hugs, always hugs. I was kinda getting irritated. I wanted a kiss! Gosh, his lips looked so luscious. Yet, I wasn't invited to touch them. So, I kept my thoughts and my tongue in check. Had to make the hug sufficient.

"So, what are we gonna do at your house?" I said with anticipation.

Tad murmured, "Trust me! It will be fun, fun, and more fun. My mother just wants to speak. Nothing serious. She's cut from a totally different mold than your mother. You can leave all the etiquette stuff in the car. Not to say my mom couldn't go there, but she's down home. Merely loves you as you are. You don't have to be what's politically correct

141

around her."

"What are you trying to say?" I asked him, looking confused. "You don't like my mother?"

"Now see, I knew you were gonna read more into it than I said," Tad explained. "We need both types of women like our moms in the world. I respect your mother a lot. Hey, Mrs. Skky has got to be great; she raised you. And I sure like you quite a bit."

He only lived about twenty-five minutes away. But the farther we drove towards the South Carolina line, the more dismal it seemed. I felt I was driving through Hickville—you know, the booneys. I saw nothing but trees and dirt. Not a store in sight.

I closed my eyes and reopened them. His world had new meaning. It was peaceful and serene. A great place to think. I definitely didn't think I could live out there, but it sure was beautiful.

As we pulled into the dirt road driveway with a little house sitting on it and three trailers around it, he said, "We don't live like you guys. But I brought you out here because I didn't think you'd care. I hope I'm not wrong."

OK, I was slightly uncomfortable. Not trying to be uppity, but I never knew anyone who lived in a trailer. It didn't look like he was poor. He had a car. Being so into enjoying his company, I simply never thought to ask him what his parents did for a living. Honestly, I didn't care. Now it seemed I was about to learn more.

The day was gray, about forty degrees or so. He parked on the brown grass in the back of the house. I stared at the clothesline in the middle of the yard. All of a sudden, four women came up to the car. At that moment, my discomfort went up another notch.

Before I could open the car door, it was being opened for me. Not by Tad. It was a girl about my age.

"Get out of there, girl," muttered a sweet lady approximately in her forties.

The cute girl who assisted in helping me out of the car said, "Chocolate, introduce us."

"Ah, she so . . . prutty," the elderly women replied, squeezing my cheeks.

"Yes, she is adorable," responded the last lady.

Tad escorted me over to the last one and said, "Payton, this is my mom. Over here is my lovely grandma, my sweet Aunt Gussie, and her daughter Gina. Gina is a junior at Silver Bluff."

Call me dumb, but all these women were light-skinned. I mean very light. Lighter than Rain. Tad is related to them. He's a pretty dark brother. Don't get me wrong; I find his color very appealing. He is absolutely gorgeous. Maybe I'm just intrigued because I've never seen a black family with such different shades. Actually, it's kind of neat.

The little house was his grandmother's, I learned. His grandfather passed ten years ago. Tad's mom is the second oldest of ten children. The three trailers that surround the house were owned by members of their family. Tad and his parents lived in one.

When we went inside the house, it was packed with people. I was amazed at how many folks could comfortably fit in it. I met Tad's first cousins, second cousins, and third cousins. Although I was introduced to everyone as Tad's friend, they treated me like I was a cousin too. I felt at home instantly.

Chitterlings, collard greens, pigs' feet, yams, black-eyed peas, ham—whatever soul food you love, it was there. I can't forget the ham hocks and the corn bread. What a spread. And to drink, well, it was the weirdest combination. Tea-co-lade is what his grandmother called it. Of course, I was skeptical. Oh, but it was great! Sweet tea, Coke, and lemonade equally mixed together.

After the meal and the talking, we went outside. It was

chilly, but Tad held my arm and pulled me near him. I cherished absorbing a whole different aspect of the earth. We strolled down the dirt road and exchanged thoughts.

When we got up the street a ways, he implied that we were looking at my surprise. I was baffled. He had to be joking. All I saw was an open field and two homemade little wagons. He corrected me and explained that they were go-carts. Then, he taught me how to ride them.

The two of us had a blast; me chasing him, and him chasing me. Then he got on the cart with me. Gosh, was that ever fun. He drove us into the middle of the cornfield. I had experienced nothing like this before. If Tad hadn't been there with me, I would have been terrified—not of the sight, but I would not have known how to get back to the dirt road.

He stared into my eyes and said, "I hope you're enjoying yourself, Payton."

"I've never been exposed to this type of fun," I told him as I got off the go-cart and shook off the dirt.

Tad seriously said, "I've got something important I want to ask you."

I thought, *Wow, here we go. He's gonna ask me to be his girl. Finally, finally, finally, the big question is here!*

But then he said what I wasn't expecting, "Next week is when I declare what college I plan to attend. Silver Bluff is having this little shindig sorta thing. Some of the coaches, family, and friends will be there. Like I told you a while ago, I do not have many true buddies. And I really dig your company. When you're around me, things are pretty cool. So, I was hoping you'd come to the press conference next Friday. It's gonna be after school."

It took me a second to respond. That wasn't what I wanted him to say, but all the same, it was still very special. What an honor for him to ask me to be there. There's no way I could turn down such an invitation.

So I uttered, "Count me in! I'll take pride in being there

for you on such a momentous occasion."

He gave me a bear grip and said, "Thanks!"

I pulled up to Silver Bluff that Friday at approximately three-fifty in the afternoon. There were tons of cars. All three of the networks had a news van at the site.

Walking through the halls of the school was complicated, being that I had never been there before. As I followed the crowd, I easily made it to the gym. That's where the press conference was being held. It was easy to spot Tad. He was up on the podium with his parents and coaches.

At his house last week, I didn't get to meet his dad. His father is a truck driver and he was on the road. I knew instantly who his dad was 'cause Tad was his clone. No wonder he resembled no one on his mother's side.

There was a large crowd of people standing on the gymnasium floor. I was right behind two girls. One was obviously infatuated with Tad. I didn't try to pry, but it wasn't hard to hear her say how badly she wanted to go out with him.

I'll have to say, she was attractive. However, the sista was in desperate need of a perm. Lord, forgive my ugly thoughts. Huh, I needed one badly last week.

"I can't believe he hasn't asked me to the prom yet. Who else is there to take?" the girl asked.

Her friend said, "I don't know, girl, but you better make your move soon. The cotillion and prom are gettin' pretty close."

Oh no, they're debs! Life gets more and more interesting by the day. I hadn't done a good job of meeting all the girls. Since they were in front of me, I had no clue if I'd met them before. Not wanting to burst their bubble about Tad, I moved to another area.

I ended up posted in back of two guys that were talking about my friend. I assumed they were Tad's teammates.

Their builds were distinct giveaways.

One, obviously jealous, said to his buddy, "Yo Champ, that brother think he all that. Gettin' a lil' scholarship. Act like he too good to talk to the brothers now. Think he can tote that mail, but his game ain't nothin.' Gon' get to the big leagues and get embarrassed. That's what's gonna go down."

I wanted to go off on him. Luckily, the other dude had Tad's back. Everybody ain't foul.

"Why you gotta be like that? A guy get a chance to get away from here and make something of himself, and what we do—talk 'im down. Man, I'm proud of 'im. Happy for 'im. Shoot, at least somebody doin' something good for a change," the Champ guy retaliated in Tad's defense.

Yeah, yeah—that's right, tell him, I wanted to say aloud. However, my attention quickly focused on the podium. I heard Tad's voice.

"First of all, I want to put this moment in perspective and thank God. Without His favor on my life, I wouldn't have been able to say I was going to anybody's college, under any circumstances," Tad professed proudly. "But to be going on scholarship is truly an awesome blessing. I'm so unworthy of it. Also, I'd like to thank my parents and family, the head coach and staff, and my teammates and friends. Without your love and support, I know I would not have made it. I won't keep you long. Cutting to the chase, I want to announce that I plan to attend the University of Georgia in Athens. This decision was an easy one. I say that because the athletic department there really believes in me. With their starting tailback a graduating senior, they have expressed sincere interest in grooming me to start next year. I plan to work hard to earn that job."

Tad went on for another few minutes. Everyone was listening intensely. His mother was smiling from here to Phoenix.

In closing he said, "I'll miss playing here at Silver Bluff.

But you better believe a piece of Silver Bluff will always be with me. If there's anyone out there that doesn't think they can make their dreams happen, I just want to encourage you that if I can do it, so can you. Settle for nothing less. As Zig Ziglar says, 'I'll see you at the top'!"

He received an ovation of cheer. Then, question and answer time, and a reception in the cafeteria. And since he was busy entertaining the media, I walked over to the lunchroom filled with balloons.

The two girls I was behind earlier saw that I was alone. After a few minutes of them whispering to each other, they strolled over to me. What did they want? I asked myself.

"Hello . . . Payton?" one girl stated with uncertainty.

I answered, "Yep, it's me. Keisha, right?"

The other girl that liked Tad said rudely, "No! Her name is Kresolyn and I'm Val."

Like I asked what her name was. And I only met Kresolyn briefly. Sue me for not remembering her name. Shucks, she wasn't even certain of mine.

Val inquired, "You attend Lucy Laney. What are you doing all the way out here, may I ask?"

The strong voice of the hour interrupted, "She's with me."

Tad grabbed my hand. Val was squirming mad. Her eyes started to tear. Tad didn't even notice. Probably never realized she had a crush on him. At that point, my heart went out to her. I know how it feels to lose a guy you want.

"I've been looking for you all over. I'm tired. Let's get out of here," Tad voiced softly in my ear.

We said bye to the girls and walked toward outside. I felt like a bouquet of red roses given to a girl on Valentine's Day, cherished and appreciated. On our way to my car, we stopped at his locker. The hall was abandoned, but being with him I felt filled.

He pulled out something in a red heart box and said, "I

got these for you. They are Godiva turtle chocolates. Now, before you say you don't like 'em, give me a chance to explain. Of the small amount of people in the world who do not like chocolate, most of them feel differently about this brand. I got you turtles because it's synonymous of our relationship. Slow, yet moving. The peanut represents the crunch. It's crunch time now! Here comes the big question. Will you be my girl, or what? If you answer yes, it will be as sweet and smooth as the caramel inside this candy in my hand."

I took the turtle from him and bit into it. Actually, it tasted pretty good. Slowly, I ate the rest.

He asked impatiently, "So?"

I said, bulging with smiles and excitement, "Yes, I'll be your girl . . . 'cause in more ways than one, I'm falling for chocolate!"

12

Studying God's Word

Kissing him that first time was more than spectacular! It might as well have been the Fourth of July instead of the middle of February. Tons of fireworks went off everywhere. My heart was pounding from my chest the precious moment his lips graced mine.

But something was missing. It was his tongue. I tried to slide mine down his mouth. However, he wouldn't gap his lips an inch to let it in.

Getting agitated at my persistence, he announced, "You know, maybe I misled you, Payton. All I wanted was a kiss. If we go any further, it's gonna lead to a whole lot of trouble. As I stare at our current surroundings, I already feel I've crossed the line. We're in my car, out here tonight, at this new construction subdivision . . . nothing out here but bricks, trees, and us. Don't get me wrong—boy, do I want you. I just can't."

"No Tad, don't pull away," I insisted, trying desperately to hold on to him. "It feels so cozy and wonderful with your arms draped around me. You can't stop the fire before it burns bright."

"I don't want a relationship like this!" he said in a loud tone.

I'm not certain whether I was angry at him or at myself; nevertheless, I got out of the car and slammed the door. It was too dark and desolate to go anywhere. Afraid, I stuck close to the car because the only lights out there were from his old Toyota. And even those weren't shining too brightly. So I leaned over the front hood.

He didn't get out of the car immediately. The time I had to myself, I just reflected. I pondered on how I got myself back in this type of situation. It was a place where I wanted desperately to be intimate with a guy. Recently, I had just vowed to God that I wouldn't tread in those waters until I rode the wave of marriage!

A one-week courtship was far from marriage. I was consumed with guilt. Knowing that I had let not only a wonderful guy down, but a holy God as well, I cried, weeping in sorrow for being so weak.

I guess when Tad saw my pain, he came to my aid. I felt too unworthy to be consoled. Didn't want him to hug me, touch me, nothing. I felt so dirty, so cheap, so filthy. I tried to walk away from his questions, but he grabbed my elbow and pulled me to him.

Hoping to shake away my hurt, he voiced with concern, "I know what's wrong. I'm sorry I pulled away—"

Before Tad could go on thinking he knew what was on my mind, I had to stop him. He didn't need to apologize. He didn't need to give in. He needed to stand strong. He needed to show me the road our relationship should take.

He was right to let his heart lead and not his loins. His heart followed God. Certainly, that's who I needed to follow.

"Payton, if you won't let me talk," he said, "then please talk to me. Let me in. How can we develop any type of relationship if we cannot communicate freely, openly, and honestly?"

Wiping my face, I gasped as I turned away from him. "You know, you never asked me why Dakari and I broke up. Maybe you figured I didn't want to discuss it because it was too personal and painful. Or you might just not care. I only know you never asked. Surely you are aware he has another girlfriend. The whole stupid town knows that."

I paused. Before I told Tad the rest, I turned back to face him. Then I got emotional.

"See, it's so deep. I lost him because I wouldn't sleep with him. I lost him because I would not have sex with him. I lost him because I couldn't give him what he wanted. Someone else gladly did. That part really tore me up."

He passionately said, "You don't have to sweat me leaving you over nothing like that. I'm not in this for sex."

"I know that. I know that," I muttered to him. "You want me to be honest? Well, here it goes. Look, even though I wasn't intimate with Dakari doesn't mean that I didn't wanna be. That is why I'm all upset with myself now. I wasn't kissing on you because of obligation, to keep you. It was because something inside of me was yearning and wanting something more."

Although what I was saying was troubling, I continued. I knew Dakari would have never cared to hear such an explanation. Then again, Dakari, the jerk, wasn't ever as sensitive to my feelings in two years as Tad had been in two months.

I uttered, "I'm so scared 'cause that part of me is in control. The Holy Spirit which resides inside of me is on the verge of eviction. Yeah, I also know I let you down, Tad. Probably made ya do some things you didn't want to do. Even more than that, I promised God I wouldn't stumble in this area. And here I am, falling right back into temptation. I don't know; I think God hates me. Rightly, He should! I went back on my word."

The next few moments were supernatural. I felt a cleansing like never before. Tad took my hands, squeezed them, and prayed.

"Father," he began, "I come to You now asking for Your heavenly forgiveness and asking You to wash away all our sins. Lord, Payton and I thank You so much for allowing our paths to cross in this world. You've trusted us with a deep friendship. I am blessed to know such a special young lady. She brings joy to my heart and soul. Father, I'm sure You allowed us to be intimate with our thoughts because You hoped it would be sufficient to sustain our relationship for now. But, Father, we really want each other. You know! Although we didn't totally break the barrier, we were knocking on the wall of sin."

As I listened to my new boyfriend pray, I was beside myself. I had never prayed with Dakari. The whole experience felt magical, anointed, and special. It was as if God was there with us, wrapping us in His arms.

"I pray, Lord, for my girlfriend," Tad spoke with his head still bowed, "as she struggles with disappointing You. Please, give her the peace that I feel showering me clean right now. Help her understand that once we ask for Your forgiveness, redemption is granted. Assist us in wanting to know You more. If we are connected to You, we won't find ourselves wavering in our faith. We know that You love us with an unending love. We also know that You are holding us accountable for what we do from this point on. Amen."

"Hey Payton, babe, God showed me how our dating can be honoring to Him and pleasing to us," Tad told me over the phone the next day.

I didn't know what Tad was thinking, but I knew something had to be done. The promises we made to God needed to be kept. I simply had no clue how that could be done.

Well, other than staying far away from Tad. And I don't think I'm quite ready to end things. It just began. As long as he was proposing any other option, I was for it.

"Tell me, what are you thinking?" I said to him very curiously.

"I think that after our prayer yesterday, it was clear that God is the center of our relationship. And if He's the center, we have to know Him more. The only way to do that is to stand on the Rock," he replied.

I asked, "Stand on the rock? I—I don't know what you mean."

"Stand on His Word, Payton. Stand on His Word," Tad explained.

I again asked, "What are you sayin'? I still don't fully understand."

Tad uttered with hope, "I don't know how you'd feel about this, but I want to start reading God's Word with you. I'm asking you to be more than my girlfriend. I want you to be my sister in Christ."

It took a minute for me to respond. Shocked! Though not in a bad way.

I responded, "Tad, I . . . I don't know what to say."

"Well, you don't have to feel obligated," he told me.

"It's not that," I said emphatically. "It's just that you're, so different from any guy I—"

My boyfriend cut me off and voiced, "Yeah, I know I'm different. Probably because I'm not just saying I'm a Christian, but I'm honestly trying to live my life as one. It's not easy. Don't misunderstand; I don't get teased, or joked on, or anything like that. Guys give me my props because of the way I ball. I try and stand my ground. Don't chug the forties at parties. Don't allow the guys to cuss around me. Don't lie and brag about bangin' women. Sure, I get teased a little. The fellas say, 'Man, you better come up off them prayers and get into them panties.' Pay it no attention

153

though. Pray for them jokers, and keep tending to my business."

Gosh, I thought, *I can really imagine him walking away from their coarse joking.* Such a strong guy. So glad God entrusted me to date him. He's rare, but he is real.

Tad continued, "I don't know where you are in your walk with Christ. But I'm asking you to come out on a limb with me and hang from the branches. The branches are connected to the vine, which is Jesus. I can only promise you one thing, and that is that it will be interesting. Thank goodness, God has stated in His Word that if we stay connected to Him, everything we have will blossom. That means our relationship will be blessed."

"I admit," I voiced to Tad, "I'm not where I need to be when it comes to serving God. Don't get me wrong; even though this is different, I do like the idea. I like it a lot. I like the feeling I felt yesterday when you prayed for us. Although new for me, it felt very comfortable. I want more of that feeling. It was more satisfying than our beloved kiss. We were as one with our thoughts to the Almighty."

We were becoming so close. I pray with my family. I pray with my girlfriends. Constantly, I pray by myself. But praying with my boyfriend. How awesome! Yeah, I'm game to read the Bible with him.

My Sunday school teacher always encourages us to get in a small study group. I've always blown the idea off. Now, though, God's blowing a chance my way. I won't run against the current any longer. This time, I'll run to His Word. Yep, I'll soak up all the Lord wants to give me.

"So when do we start?" I asked him.

"Well," Tad took a breath and replied, "tomorrow is Valentine's Day. I know we planned to go to dinner with your parents. I was thinking after the meal, when we get back to your place, we could start then. It may sound somewhat corny, but trust me, it'll be cool. Our first Valentine's will be all that!"

_____

Later that afternoon, I was coolin' out at the mall with my friends. All of us were trying to pick out something cute to wear for Valentine's. In addition to shopping, we also sat in the food court and gabbed.

"So, what do you and Tad got going?" Lynzi asked nosily.

Last week they were all so excited for me when I told them Tad had asked me to go with him. The four of us were trying to keep it hush-hush around school. We figured it was no one's business to know how happy I was with my new fella.

Well, I take that back; Dymond didn't think I really liked Tad. She wrongfully assumed I was just trying to get back at Dakari. At first I didn't like Tad—true enough. But as the months passed, so did my feelings for Dakari. Then the door was open to receive another special guy in my life. Somehow, some way, luckily I should say, I realized Tad had the qualities I needed in a boyfriend.

"Ah, we're planning a nice evening," I uttered, cutting it short.

I hoped they would then go on to the next person. You see, I was very timid about telling them my plans. First of all, dinner with my parents, my brother, and his girlfriend isn't very romantic. Secondly, I didn't feel they'd understand about the Bible thing. Honestly, I wasn't fully sure how fun it would be either.

Getting into God's Word sounds rather boring. Surely the girls would have thought that. So I didn't let them in on it. Maybe I should have.

Dinner was turning out to be better than I had imagined. The six of us dined at a Chinese restaurant by candlelight. My parents weren't overbearing. They were relaxed and cool. Perry was happy because, since he was only fifteen, he's only allowed to date during the summer. So, if my parents wouldn't have agreed to take us out, Perry wouldn't have gotten to see Tori on Valentine's.

All during the meal I was thinking about what was to come. This Bible study thing was beginning to scare me. What if he asked me to turn to Deuteronomy. I'm ashamed to say, I don't know where that is. Actually, that's all the more reason why I need to be doing this.

When we got home, my family gave Tad and me some privacy in the den. Before we said any words, we pulled out our presents and we exchanged gifts. I bought him a cute, sporty outfit from Structure. I guessed on the size. Assumed he could exchange it with no problem if it didn't fit.

Next, he handed me a box and said, "This is a little something to keep you on the right page."

Earlier, he had given me six red roses when he came to the house. I guess somewhere along the way I had told him that I loved them.

I opened the tiny red box, carefully tied with white ribbon. Unlike Tad. He had ripped through his paper. It was pretty cool to find a 14-karat-gold bookmark. To make it extra special, the marker was engraved. It read: "To my dearest Payton, May you continually press towards the highest mark. You deserve the best God's got to give. Always, Tad."

"This is so sweet," I said to him as I gave him a hug. "Thank you."

Next he handed me a gift bag. Without hesitation, I removed the crepe paper to get to the third gift. It was a book. The title was, *Dating: Guidelines from the Bible.*

"Wow, this seems interesting," I voiced to Tad with appreciation.

He reached behind his seat and pulled out another copy of the book. It wasn't a thick novel. The cover appeared rather cozy.

He said, "I've already read the book once. The words were like food to my hungry spirit. I hope you get a chance to read it all. But tonight, I want us to focus on two chapters. One is chapter six. 'What makes a good dating relationship' is the topic. The other is 'How to keep from going too far,' chapter nine."

Tad was fired up as he described his feelings for the material. He told me that the author, Scott Kirby, was also from Georgia. This book was recommended by his pastor. Tad's church youth group was about to start reading it.

It was unfortunate to hear that Tad had to go to three different secular bookstores to locate material on Christian dating. Even then, his search proved unsuccessful. Tons of books on how to do it, which way to do it, with whom to do it, etc., but not a single piece of literature on "not doing it" until marriage. Guess we need to write the bookstores and request the positive stuff.

"So, where did you find this?" I asked.

Tad answered, "At the Christian bookstore. Payton, I've got to take you there sometime soon. They've got so much good information. Lots of books on teen issues. Babe, I tell you, I had just as much fun checkin' thangs out in that store as I do in a music store."

First we dove into the things that make a great relationship. There were some essential points. One was making sure both people loved God. Psalm 119:63 says, "I am a companion of all them that fear thee." Well, we did have that going for us.

The second point was having the relationship OKed by parents. We found a few Scriptures that supported that claim: Ephesians 6:1, Colossians 3:20, and Luke 2:51. But the commandment "Honor thy father and mother" spoke volumes. We were happy to report that our parents were in support of us spending time together.

Being involved with someone who helps build you up was the next issue. One who builds up your self-esteem and builds up your walk with Christ. In I Timothy 5:1–2 the apostle Paul tells Timothy to see people as your brothers and sisters in Christ. It was comforting to us both to know that doing this study was proof of how much we truly were committed to honoring God. Not just in our dating relationship, but in all that we do. Before we moved on to the final issue, we vowed not to hinder each other spiritually.

We both knew that in order to fulfill that commitment our relationship would have to stay morally pure. Dating God's way was the final point in this chapter. I always knew God wanted me to stay a virgin. Honestly, at times it seemed like the Lord was making an unfair request. However, we were led to passages that contradicted that fact. Psalm 84:11 stood out the most as it read, "No good thing will he withhold from them that walk uprightly."

Tad said, "That verse tells me that if we follow God's plan for our lives, He will always give us what we need. We don't have to rush the course. Although, I must say I often dream of being at the finish line with you. We just gotta keep those feelings in check."

I agreed! How could I disagree—it was right there in the Bible. How could any Christian doubt that God wouldn't hold up His end of the bargain?

I found it to be pretty interesting that after each chapter there were discussion questions. That made it easier for us to talk. I enjoyed the interaction. We weren't talking just about each other. We were talking about God and us.

"Man, this is good. Let's hit chapter nine and see what's up with it!" Tad spoke in a cool and exciting way.

Before we read, he asked me a question. He asked, "What do you think could keep us from going too far?"

I was stumped. However, I took a deep breath and said, "Pray! You help me . . . I help you! Set standards! Avoid tempting situations."

I was glad Tad agreed with me. I was even more amazed that those issues were all addressed in the book. Chapter nine enlightened us. More importantly, it challenged us.

Before closing our study in prayer, we did something awesome. Tad and I claimed a Scripture to be our armor when we needed protection from ourselves. Galatians 5:16 says, "Walk in the Spirit, and ye shall not fulfill the lust of the flesh."

As I walked this guy I admired so much to the door, we embraced. The hug was one of pride. We felt good that our dating relationship was now being built correctly. We were no longer building with straw, which is lust. We were no longer building with sticks, which is peer pressure. We were building with bricks, which is God's Word. Sound biblical principles we could use in a fun, positive, and uplifting way to honor the Lord and please all three of us.

After church the next day, the girls came over for a study session. Even though we had Pre-Calculus at different times, we all had the same teacher. Mrs. Starghill's test had each of us in knots. It was tomorrow, and I was not ready.

"Dy, help explain this problem to me," I asked as I handed her my notebook.

Dymond said, "OK, just hold up a minute. I'm tryin' to figure it out myself."

"You? stumped?" Lynzi uttered. "Now I know we need a break. Put down the book. Let's chat. How was your Valentine's? Mine was great."

Lynzi went on to share what a wonderful time she and

Bam had at the Jazz club. Bam gave her a cashmere sweater. It was adorable. Of course, she brought it to showoff.

Rain and Tyson spent their evening at a private restaurant in Historic Augusta. They rode around in a limo. Tyson won the sweetheart night dream ride through a slam dunk contest the radio station was sponsoring.

The Country Buffet is where Dymond and Fatz had their date. She claimed they had the best time. I guess what was so special was that this "all you can eat" place is their favorite restaurant. Even though their dining choice would have never been mine, I did think the 14-karat-gold locket with his picture in it was a very romantic gift.

"Tell us 'bout your night, Payton," Lynzi said.

Suddenly I didn't care what they thought as I uttered, "Well, it wasn't the type of date that was romantic in the traditional sense. Although, I did receive six of my favorite color roses. It was much more meaningful. We found out a lot about each other, and I thought I already knew this guy so well. But last night, I saw an even more precious side of him. That's a side . . . a side that loves God. It might sound boring to you guys, but it's wonderful to me. I mean, 'cause if he loves God, then Tad has room to love and respect me. Jesus was the center of our date. The Lord blessed us too. He showed Tad and me that there is joy in honoring Him. God showed me that it is cool to learn more about Him. It was definitely a Valentine's Day I'll never forget. Our date was full of intimacy, as we opened up the Bible and enjoyed studying God's Word."

13

Practicing Every Move

"Six o'clock seems like it's never gonna roll around," Lynzi sighed as she stared at her watch. "I'll be so glad when the guys get here and we get to check out everybody's escort."

The forum on "Special Concerns for Young Women" was rather interesting. We covered a wide range of topics. Some were serious and some were fun.

Date violence was an issue that we tackled for a while. It was surprising to find that half of us admitted to being in some type of abusive situations with a guy. I commend the Links panel on their advice and counsel in that area. "If your date hits you once, don't date him again under any circumstances" was the point the older ladies kept emphasizing.

It was great when Dymond broke the melancholy atmosphere and voiced her concern. She's silly anyway. But, with all the sad abuse stories, we needed to laugh and move on.

Dymond explained with a serious expression, "Don't ya'll laugh now, but I've got a very important special concern. I'm expecting my cycle during the week of the cotillion. We're wearing white dresses and—"

She had to speak no further. Bursts of laughter filled the place. Obviously, a room full of ladies could totally relate. Quite a few other girls stood up as well and admitted they were in the same predicament. It was very clear that topic needed to be addressed in a major way. We vowed to watch each other from behind closely during the ceremony in May. Also, we were advised to freshen up whenever possible on that night.

After the forum in a small room at the Civic Center, we all headed over to the banquet hall a few rooms down. This was to be the first practice for the ball. The fifty of us knew each other kinda well. The slumber party was a huge success last weekend. Most of the time, everyone bragged on their escorts.

Finally, the time was here to meet the men of mystery. Everyone was wondering about everyone else's date. All of the gentlemen were supposed to report promptly after our meeting.

So, when the forum let out there was a mad dash for the ladies' room. Knowing that the guys were in the next room, we all wanted to look our best.

Starr was the worst primping gal I'd ever seen. Miss Thang pushed her way to the front mirror and bumped into me, saying, "Oh Payton, I can't wait to see your date. Well, that is, if you've found one yet."

When she had the audacity to be so bold and cruel, I knew the evening was going to be fun. I just kinda smiled and walked away. I guess since she snatched one guy from me, Starr was confident that I could not land another catch.

When I strolled out of the ladies' room, Dymond, Lynzi, and Rain were huddled waiting on me. We walked into the ballroom together. Each of our heads focused on the side where the guys were sitting.

It was a weird setup. All the debs had to sit on the right and all the escorts were on the left. Something about when they lined us up it would be easier. None of us thought that made sense, but we didn't argue. We knew obeying the rules was a part of being a deb.

Velda Flannery was our Movement Coordinator. She's a professional dancer. We were told that Ms. Flannery dances on Broadway. The guys didn't seem impressed until they saw her. She was a drop-dead gorgeous, all-that Lela Rochon clone. The boys let out a few cheers for her when Velda named some videos she was in.

This was the first time that the Links had secured her services. I think the ladies were nervous. After all, she was responsible for coordinating every routine.

Last year, the debs complained that the old instructor was not hip enough. That woman was sixty-six. She could hardly twirl, much less teach anybody to waltz. Velda, on the other hand—well, let's just say this twenty-five-year-old was the total opposite. And after having hired her, the Links could only hope for the best from her work.

I glanced all around, looking to the other side for Tad. I didn't see him. That made me worry. I knew he'd show up. Just hoped nothing came up to detain him.

The finest guys in this section of the South were in attendance. Maybe that's exaggerating it a bit. The big discussion was whose date had it going on the most.

Then I heard a bunch of girls going crazy over somebody. Dymond went in the midst of their discussion to see who was the lucky beau. She called my name and pointed to the person way back in the corner. When I looked at him, my heart fluttered. It was Tad that drew the attention.

I couldn't believe it when I heard Dakari's girlfriend blab, "Whose ever date that is, might as well get ready . . . 'cause I'm going after him."

"Not in this lifetime," I said to myself. Most definitely not

163

twice with my man. Plus, I knew that what she had, Tad didn't need. Besides what she had was all used up by Dakari and who knows who else.

Ms. Flannery—Velda is what she wanted to be called—shouted out, "OK girls, line up, shortest to tallest."

We quickly obeyed. The simple task took about twenty minutes. Girls bickering about who's taller, who's shorter. Finally, Velda stepped in and put us in place.

Then she said, "All right, gentlemen, find your debutante and stand to the left of her, please."

I was amazed at how many girls were following Tad's movement with their eyes. Being nosy! Trying to see who he was gonna stand beside. See, there were only two girls in the ball from South Carolina. So, Mr. Taylor was very intriguing to most.

Before he got to his destination, Velda put Starr right behind me and said, "Honey, you are not that tall. Yep, this is where you belong."

I uttered under my breath, "WHY ME?"

Dakari stood by her first. A small part of me felt sick. Hearing him carry on was a little much. I hadn't heard his soft, warm voice in so long. This semester we had no classes together.

Tad was addressed just before he got in line as Dakari said, "Hey man, what's up? I didn't know you were in this thing too. Where's your girl?"

"Yeah, where is your girl?" Starr said interrupting the guys' conversation.

"I don't know," Tad voiced in confusion. "I can't find her."

All he could see was the back of my head. I was facing forward holding my breath, because I knew the fireworks were about to begin.

Turning to them I said, "Here I am babe—right here."

I reached out my hand and pulled Tad to me. Both

Dakari and Starr's mouth just fell to the ground. It was a Kodak moment. As Tad got in line and hugged me, I heard Dakari breathe a sigh of disappointment. It was obvious that he was jealous. I already knew he didn't like Tad. Word had gotten around that the University of Georgia had rescinded their scholarship offer to Dakari. Supposedly, he was told that since they had signed the halfback they wanted, the remainder of their scholarships would be used to secure other positions.

"Payton, hey lady," Dakari said to me. "I didn't realize you knew Tad."

I replied with excitement, "Yeah . . . remember, you introduced me to him at the first University of Georgia game last year."

"Well, Miss Skky, I'd like to meet your beau. I mean, date," Starr responded in a slick way.

"Starr, this is my BOYFRIEND, Tad Taylor. Sweetie, this is Starr Love, Dakari's girlfriend. Isn't he a lucky guy?" I asked sarcastically.

Starr held her hand out to shake his. Tad just kinda waved from a distance. Then he grabbed my hand and turned around. It was so cool. The attention she's used to getting from every guy who sees her was not going to be given by my man. Well, not this man anyway.

Velda started practice after the order was recorded. We learned one dance, which was the fun finale. It was cool that girls stopped me to give me props on my escort. Being with Tad was great. We were in a world all our own. I was beginning to look forward to the cotillion I had so dreaded in the past.

The next Tuesday rehearsal, Tad picked me up for practice. I had just gotten home from working on SGA elections. So, while I was getting ready, my mother entertained him.

165

They sipped peppermint tea and nibbled buttermilk muffins. The way she drilled him was adorable.

I could hear her inquisitive voice from upstairs saying, "Tad dear, have you ever attended a debutante ball?

"No ma'am," Tad answered carefully, "but I can say I've heard quite a bit about them from my family. All of my aunts are really excited that I'm going to be participating. And with the fun I had last week at practice, I'm getting pumped for the big event. In addition to that, Payton has told me how important this cotillion is to you. Therefore, please know that I'll do my best to meet your every expectation."

"Well, I must say," my mother responded in an impressed tone, "ever since my daughter started accompanying me to deb-related activities, I've always hoped and prayed she'd be a debutante. Now that Payton is a participant, my concern has shifted. My desire for her is that she grows from and enjoys the experience. Having a proper escort aids in both of those things. You see, in past years I've run across some real characters. Those young boys were everything but what an escort should be. After speaking with you on this issue, I am very confident my daughter will be with a perfect gentleman. It would be an extra bonus if every girl involved this year could be so lucky!"

When we headed out the door, Tad grabbed my coat. He then assisted me in putting it on. Adding to his politeness, he opened not only the front door for me, but the car door as well. Yep, my mother was really impressed. So was I, actually. So was I!

"What are you thinking?" Tad asked me as we were about halfway to the Civic Center.

"Umm, to be honest," I replied, staring passionately at the guy I was falling deeper for every day, "when I broke up with Dakari, it was so tough. I can't even explain my heartache. I felt God had left me. Now, I know that He took me through that pain for a greater pleasure. For if that had never happened to me—you know, me gettin' dumped—I never would have found my way to you. It just proves the verse "Great is Thy faithfulness."

When we arrived on the ballroom floor, Rain and Tyson walked up to us. I was thrilled that he and Tad had hit it off so well. Luckily, Tad never held the defeat in the Christmas tournament against Tyson. Tad is such a sportsman. He admires Tyson's skills. Of course, Rain and I used the minute to give each other the scoop on our day.

Practice was even better than last week. Everyone was getting along. Velda kept crackin' us up with her stickler ways. Ms. Flannery was determined to have us ready.

There was one couple—bless their hearts—they were so uncoordinated. If Eugene went one way, Sally would have to go the other. It was neat how a lot of people traded off, trying to show them the movements in slow motion.

Unfortunately, the Tuesday that followed was hardly similar to the one before. Seemed like everyone showed up with attitudes. To top it off, Velda had the worst one.

It was obvious that she wanted to make this the best debutante ball ever. Okay, that fact was cool with most of us. Being remembered as the class of girls with the coolest cotillion in Augusta. However, the problem came in when sweet Velda turned into Drill Sergeant Flannery. This lady wanted it to be the best ball in the United States. We were astonished when she said she had thirty-two tapes of balls from last year alone.

"You people are not giving me 100 percent. I cannot work miracles with a lazy bunch. Crunch time is here. The countdown has begun. The sand in the hourglass is running out. I'll pull you from numbers if I have to," Velda said hastily as she pointed at the door. "Now, next week for a change of pace, I want to work with just the debs. Girls, we have to practice on your solo number. Escorts, go home, regroup, and come back revived next Thursday."

"Oh, I don't care what you say, I'm gonna get Tad Taylor," I overheard Starr say as I opened the door to the ladies' room.

I couldn't believe what I was hearing. Starr Love again on the move for my guy. She is too bold.

"Lord," I prayed, "please fill me with Your spirit . . . right now. I'm so close to—"

Before I could finish my thoughts to God, Starr yelled, "Yeah, right Cuz, like I'm really sweatin' Payton. She's cute, smart, and all. But that's pretty much where the fun and perks end when it comes to what she can offer a man."

"If you've got something to say about me, turn around and say it to my face," I voiced sternly, surprising them both.

Summer tried to cover for her, as she stumbled over her words saying, "No . . . no, umm . . . she . . . we . . . we weren't talking about you."

"Thanks Cuz, but I can handle this. I ain't got no problem tellin' Miss Thang what I feel." Starr stepped in front of her and confronted me. "Your first boyfriend was fun for a while. Now, I'm tired of him. But, this new beau of yours, he's got it goin' on. And if you think you can keep him, think again!"

Rudely, Starr brushed by me and stormed out of the ladies' room. I felt like snatching her back and demanding respect. The Holy Spirit responded to my earlier call and contained my emotions.

Summer just looked at me. It was a weird stare. Seemed like she was disappointed with her cousin too. Boy, was that vibe weird. I guess she could clearly read my eyes, as they displayed how angry and upset I was. Yet, a part of me felt, Why should I worry? Tad won't stray. I should know.

Summer finally spoke, saying, "I'm really sorry about my cousin and her horrible attitude. When she first came to Augusta last summer, I wanted to be cool with her. I assumed the best way to make her like me was to be just like her. That meant I had to be down with what she is and do what she does. In confidence, I want to tell you that I made the mistake of going after someone else's guy. Only to later be hurt. Payton, I ended up really liking the dude. Through dealing with me, he found out he'd rather stick with his girlfriend. I can't divulge who he is. You understand?"

I already knew who she was describing. To spare her embarrassment, I just played it off. Bam! Yep, remember, I overheard her carrying on about him at our first deb meeting. Lynzi never said anything to either of them. When things got better between her and Bam, she just dropped the whole thing. So, I figured Summer assumed none of us knew of her fling.

Summer continued in a serious tone. "I guess I learned a very valuable lesson. That is, you don't mess with other people's relationships. That kinda stuff comes back on you. I've been trying to tell my cousin that. Unfortunately, she could care less about the repercussions. Starr thinks she can get what she wants. Period. The end."

Boy, did I ever agree. Starr is such a jerk. She has no feelings. Simply coldhearted.

"Payton," Summer stated in a sweet tone, "I know we haven't ever been good friends. Probably because I was always jealous of you. Your dad is loaded. You're adorable. Extremely popular in school. Also, you—"

I was thankful for her praise. However, I felt she was equally blessed, so I interrupted, "You've got all those things too, Summer."

"Yeah, but you're beautiful within and I guess now I know . . . that's a trait I never possessed."

She became transparent with me. Oddly, a girl I've known for years as a person on top had just revealed that her struggles are as real as anyone else's. My heart was pounding. I was bursting to show her God's love.

I touched her shoulder and expressed with compassion, "That's one thing that you can develop. Summer, based on this conversation we're having right now, I already see signs that you're changing. It takes practice to be truly good at heart. But, God's Word holds me accountable. The Bible says, 'Whatsoever a man thinketh, so is he.' So, I try to think on good things. Believe me, though, I often fall short."

Summer said slowly after pondering my words, "I really appreciate you being open and honest. I hope that we can forget things of the past and be friends."

"I'd like that," I told her smiling from the inside out. "Yeah, I'd like that a lot. One can never have too many friends."

As we strolled out of the ladies' room truly unified, she gasped with a stern face, "Watch out for my cousin. Don't misunderstand. I do love her, but I know Starr too well. She's on a mission to get Tad."

It was March twentieth and another practice was yet upon us. Since the cotillion was exactly two weeks away and Velda didn't think the group was close to ready, she added to our already busy rehearsal time. And that was a bit much. Not just Tuesdays and Thursdays anymore, but Wednesdays also. Everyone tried to argue that it was too much. Ms. Flannery compromised and agreed to allow everyone one courtesy miss. Miss two practices and you're out.

When people were out, their partner had to practice with someone there. That way we still could learn and master the steps. Velda then wanted that person who attended to later get with their real partner before the next practice and show him or her what we went over.

Well, Dakari was absent this time. Word was that he was at the doctor. I didn't give much thought to what could possibly be wrong with him because my main focus was on Starr. I needed desperately, like a heart patient needs his pacemaker, to know what was on Miss Love's mind. It was more than evident that when she asked Tad to help her learn the steps, she was up to no good. It felt as if she was a vampire waiting to suck his blood.

Before Tad agreed to assist her, he turned toward me. My sweet guy asked me if I would be OK with it. I was about to say, "No way, no day, never!"

However, Velda cut in right as I was about to open my lips and she said, "Yes, yes, yes, dear, you must be a gentleman and help Starr out. Everyone has to learn the steps."

Before I knew it, Velda had moved Tad from my side and placed him arm in arm with that girl. They waltzed off far away from me. The first few minutes of this were tolerable. Tad, though across the room, kept his eyes on me. He looked as uncomfortable as I felt.

Then something happened. Starr stared at me with the most evil glare I had ever seen. Truly it frightened me. She slid closer and closer to my guy with her embrace. Next he began laughing as she blew some tacky words, I'm sure, in his ear. I caught him crackin' a grin.

Boy, was I going crazy. What were they chatting on and on about? What was so funny? What was he thinking of her?

As even more weird thoughts went through my mind, I lost them in the crowd. After about five minutes of searching for them, something in my gut told me to step in the hall. So, I left the ballroom and followed my instinct. To no avail, I saw a sight that bothered me: Starr walking joyously alone, back towards the room.

She yelled, "Ah yeah!"

Starr looked up and saw me. We were about twenty feet apart. Both of us stopped moving. Suddenly, Starr casually got in my face.

She said, "I told you it wouldn't be long before what was yours was mine . . . again! Miss Skky, ha, ha, ha. I should have that last name. You do it no justice. With me, sky is truly the limit. But then on the other hand, Love fits pretty good too."

"Don't play," I boldly told her. "What you tryin' to say?"

Starr uttered with a straight face, "Your dear Tad and I just locked lips. And believe me, babe, he enjoyed it. You just can't keep 'em, huh? He was supposed to be showing me the routine. Ha, ha, ha. Yeah, he showed me that and some. I guess you can simply say we were practicing every move!"

14

Seeking Another Chance

No way was I hearing Starr correctly. No way had Tad forsaken our relationship. No way had I been beaten out by the same girl twice. There was just no way that I could accept any of this.

Yet with all that doubt running rampant in my mind, it was so easy to envision Tad wanting her. Even I had to honestly admit that Starr was gorgeous on the outside. However, I knew Tad had a heart to see more than just her outer beauty. Surely he could see Starr for what she really was.

I couldn't respond to Starr's bold statement. I could only focus on the horrible thought of Tad kissing her. The more I pondered on that thought, the more real it became to me. I couldn't go back in there to practice. I had to leave. So, I dashed through the hallway and out the front door. Luckily, I didn't bring a purse and my keys were on me.

When I got to my car, anger, rage, and resentment filled my hands. I was so jittery that I couldn't control my fingers enough to open the door. Everything that could go wrong was going wrong. Murphy's Law was surely happening to me. Even pressing the button on the keypad wasn't working. Then out of even more frustration, I dropped my keys.

As I started down, I saw a shadow kneeling over my key chain. Looking closer, I saw that it was Dakari. His eyes were full of tears.

"I was about to go in," he said, handing my keys back to me.

"What—what are you doing here? I thought you had some doctor's appointment or something," I questioned him, on the verge of tears myself.

For a moment, we just stood there. Guard up! Fence gated! Door bolted! Then the tear that had mounted in his eye finally dropped.

"What's wrong?" I asked him with compassion, as I placed my hand on his face to wipe his tears.

"I was about to go inside and go off on somebody. But, I think you're just what I need. I need to talk, Payton. Yeah, I know I don't deserve even a second of your precious time. Hey, I need to be bold and ask you anyway. Please," Dakari begged.

How could I say no to that face? We went over and sat in his car. I didn't have a clue what he wanted to chat with me about. After all, it had been ages. It was weird. I truly believed he was totally out of my system. However, it was evident to me that I still cared enough to want to help him out of this depressed state.

His eyes spoke volumes of pain when his lips murmured, "Payton, my life hasn't been the same since we broke up. I mean, I know it was on me and all. The way I did you was wrong. At the time, I didn't even sweat it. As I look back, though, I realize more and more I shouldn't have hurt you that way. I shouldn't have left you that way. I shouldn't have been such a jerk. I honestly believe some of the bad things that have been happening to me lately are a direct reflection of how I did you. My mom always refers to the Bible verse 'You reap what you sow.' Guess I wasn't listening hard enough."

He paused. Holding his head down, more tears rolled from his face. I wanted to embrace him and say, "It's OK!" However, he mustered up enough strength to continue.

"I didn't deserve to prosper. And Payton, I haven't. I can't correct what I did, but I can say...I can say, 'I'm sorry,' and mean it. I know you got another dude and all. Hey, the brother seems to be coming correct. But, I just want to tell you that I am finally aware of what I lost in you. If there's any way that I could take the bad back, I would. I would in a minute. We'd be together."

I didn't need to hear that. Dakari was confusing me more. Just told him I had to go. Jumped out of his car. Got in mine. And sped off!

About twenty minutes had passed. I was simply cruising home when I happened to notice Dakari following me in my rearview mirror. He started blowing his horn.

"What does he want!" I uttered. "Got some nerve running me down."

He pulled to my side and motioned for me to let down my window. I was hesitant. So many crazy things had happened already. Didn't need another bad twist. Besides I thought he had said all he needed to say. What more could there be?

"Pull...over," he shouted as the wind trailed his words. "Pull over, please!"

I was very close to Howard's Barbecue. So, I drove for about a mile and then pulled into the parking lot. Dakari followed. In the back of my mind I kept saying, "You're crazy."

I didn't get out of the car. Figured I could just tell him I had to go home. Nothing felt comfortable about this situation.

175

Dakari got out of his car and came over to mine. He tapped on my window. I had never seen him like this. He had never been so adamant in talking to me about anything. He had never seemed to need me so desperately. Never needed me to drop everything for him.

Before I got out I prayed silently, "Lord, I don't know what's going on here. To be honest, not that You don't know my thoughts anyway, a part of me likes this pursuit. So, already I'm headed for trouble. I'm committed to someone else. Even though Tad isn't honoring our commitment, help me to stay focused. Not focused on any particular guy, but focused on You. Guys are unpredictable! You are constantly there."

I stepped out of my jeep and said, "OK, you're committed to somebody. I'm committed to somebody. There is nothing else to say. So, I'm gonna hop back in my ride and leave. Don't follow me. Don't call me. Don't track me down. There's nothing else to say."

Clearly, I was shaken up. I don't really know why. Thought I knew where my life was going. Thought I knew who I was happy with. Thought I knew who I could live without. And in one day, everything—maybe—changed.

Dakari said, "Wait a minute! Hold up! First of all, Starr and I are having major problems. We've been having problems for a while. Ever since last October, she's been confronting me about my feelings for you. Starr has always been jealous of you. She hated that I compared her to you constantly. I didn't mean to, but the intimacy, the closeness, the warmth with her was absent. I could talk all day about what's wrong between me and Starr. Believe me, it's a bunch wrong. But I'll spare you the drama."

A part of me wanted to know all the gory details. Seemed like sweet revenge that their relationship wasn't "all that." I do remember, though, when Starr called me last October, prying for information. However, another side felt bad for Dakari. Truthfully, his strong actions were unsettling.

"You seem a bit frightened," Dakari expressed with a weird look on his face. "I don't know whether you're frightened of what I'm sayin' or frightened of what you're feelin.' But . . . I'll give you time to think on it. I'll give you space so you can digest all this. Call me when you want to talk."

Dakari then got in his ride and drove away. I don't know if I was frightened and all, but I will say I was most definitely overwhelmed. It look me a minute to gain composure and finally leave Howard's parking lot.

"Oh brother," I said to myself as I pulled into my driveway and saw Tad's car.

I knew he must have been inside talking with my mom. I realized it couldn't be my father 'cause he was still at work. Such a workaholic! He'll be at the dealership from nine to nine. He believes that no one can run his shop like he can.

As I got closer to the house, I heard voices. The sounds were coming from the backyard. So, I went around there. That's where I found Tad. He and Perry were standing on the deck having a man-to-man.

"Hey, there you are," Tad spoke with concern when he saw me. "What happened to you?"

"You know what, Tad?" I stated while throwing up my hand and trotting by him, "I don't even have time for this. It's late and I do not feel like discussing it. So, just please go."

"What—what," I heard him say, before I slammed the door.

A week went past, and boy, what a crazy week it was! Dakari was calling to try and get me back, while Tad kept

177

calling to see what was wrong. Me, well, I was simply trying to get away from them both.

My girls and I were driving to practice. Let me ask you,
have you ever been behind the wheel of a car driving, but
thinking of something other than the road? Well, that was
me that day. Totally dreading the practice. I'm surprised we
didn't have an accident.

I was in another world till Dy said, "Ooh, you know
word is out all over school that Dakari wants you back.
What ya gon' do girl?"

I just laughed on the inside and kept silent on the outside. The nerve of Dakari thinking he can have me back,
just like that. Uh, I don't think so.

Rain said, "She could care less about Da—Kari. My girl
has a man. A real man that would never do her wrong. She
ain't halfway studdin' Mr. Graham."

Still I said nothing. I mean, Tad got everyone thinking
he's all innocent. Yet, the moment some floozy lifts her skirt,
bats her eye, whispers come here, he is there. Nope, I'm not
having that mess either.

The three of them were talking about how excited they
were getting over the cotillion and the prom. I could not
participate in that moment. You see, I was no longer looking forward to either.

Shucks, I didn't even know if Tad was going to show up
for rehearsal. After all, we hadn't spoken all week. I
unplugged my answering machine so there could be no
messages for me to return. Surely Tad and probably Dakari,
too, were mad at me. But I didn't care.

We had been at the Civic Center for about thirty minutes. Tad was nowhere in sight. Just when we were about to
start practicing, he walked through the door.

He came up to me and quietly said in my ear, "I don't
know what's up with you. But hey, obviously you don't
care that I'm concerned. So, as of right now, consider me

concerned no more. I'm only here because I gave my word that I'd escort you. I won't bail on that."

His brash and cold tone kinda hurt my feelings. Tad put it off on me. Like I was the one who kissed Starr? NOT EVEN!

We just went through practice not saying a word to each other. Dakari tried to rap, but I just ignored him. Every time Starr danced my way, I wanted to smack her. I know that's wrong, but I felt she's responsible for all this drama in my life. Who knows, though? Maybe I would have had these problems without her. Doubt it!

"So baby," Dakari said to me, after school, two and a half weeks later, "I've left you alone for a while. Now, I'm asking for a favor."

"Which is?" I replied kinda antsy being that it was about to rain.

He began, "Well, you know tomorrow is the draft?"

"No, I don't know," I responded. "What draft?"

"The NFL draft," Dakari told me. "My folks are having this little set for Drake. His girl, Hayli, is coming down. Our grandparents will be over. Some of his buddies from UGA are gonna come and support him. They said I could invite some of my friends as well. However, I don't want to invite anybody but you. I mean, I'm not asking you to come as my girl. I'm asking you to come as my friend. It's kinda tough for me. Ever since we were in little league, my pops has been hyped on us going pro. Now my big brother is just a step away from fulfilling that dream. I don't even know if I'll get playing time in college, much less play in the National Football League."

He paused. Then he looked away. The thunder I heard from the sky sounded just as sharp as the cry in his voice. I saw the shame in his eyes. His pain touched me.

"It's not that I'm not happy for Drake and all. I am, but
. . . You're just the only one that understands. I know you
can help me through this tough day. Please, Payton, don't
say no. I realize I do not deserve to have you there. Believe
me, I need you there."

I sighed and uttered, "What time?"

"Ah man, you'll come. Grrreat! The draft starts at noon.
Come any time around then. I can't say, umm . . . how much
I appreciate this," Dakari said with a smile.

"And who is all supposed to be at this party?" I questioned Rain as we pulled to Tyson's house.

You see, Tyson had recently declared that he was going
to Georgia Tech in the fall. They gave him a full four-year
scholarship for basketball. He has a 2.3 GPA, so honestly I
was surprised that they wanted him. Now, I simply hope
Tyson can cut it there academically. But, when you can ball
like "Air Tyson," I guess the school will make certain he
hangs in and receives the grades he needs to stay. Of course,
Rain was ecstatic, because with her attending Spelman,
they'd be in Atlanta near each other.

"It was just supposed to be a few people," Rain replied.
"I don't know how all these people found out. Look at all
these cars. Dang, these crazy folks even parked on his
grass."

I knew Lynzi and Dymond were gonna be there with
their guys. We all talked about it at school earlier. But, shoot,
I really wasn't up for a big bash. However, it wasn't my party.
So, I was just gonna have to suck up the long face and deal
with it. I hadn't planned on coming, but Rain convinced me.
Surely, I could put up with whoever for a couple of hours.

"Hey, come on in, ladies," Tyson said at the door.

The music was blasting. People were everywhere. And
tons of food was all over the house.

Tyson's mom, Shirley, was in the midst of it all. She was happy that her baby was going to college. Her beauty salon was extremely successful; however, she doesn't have a degree to her name. Well, not unless you count a beauty school certificate. Shirley always brags that Tyson is going to be the first in her family to get a college degree.

Yep, she was excited. 'Cause folks were standing on her tables and couches and she wasn't even mad. I thought it was awesome to see her so proud.

Lynzi tapped me on the shoulder and blabbed, "Hey girlfriend, you look cute tonight. So does that sista hangin' all over yo' man."

Lynzi quickly turned my head towards outside. That is where I clearly saw Tad and some chick with a bad hair weave dancing way too close to him. Never had I ever seen this chick. I don't know whether or not I had the right, but I was jealous.

My mouth hung open. What really could I say, though? Basically, Tad and I hadn't spoken in almost two weeks. Yet, as soon as I saw him in the arms of another, I realized my feelings for him were still very strong.

As soon as he saw me, he quickly left the girl and came toward me. Before he got to my side, I turned away. However, Tad grabbed my arm so I could not move.

He said, "What's your problem, Payton? Why can't you face me? Why you trippin'?"

"AS IF YOU DON'T KNOW!" I screamed, louder than the music.

People started staring at us. They could tell there was tension. I was so confused.

Tad calmed me down with his measured voice. "May I please speak with you alone?"

Neither of us knew Tyson's house that well. After opening five closed doors, we finally found a bathroom that no one was in. Even angry, Tad looked fine. But, I couldn't let my heart distract me from what my head knew to be true. He was a dog. Just like every other guy. So, there was nothing he could say that would make me forget why I was mad at him.

"All I have to say is: Starr! You should know the rest. Don't even stand in front of me and play innocent," I blurted out in a demanding voice.

"Starr? Starr what? What about her? You know, she said something to me about an early April Fools' joke that she played on you," Tad stated. "Starr told me that she got you good. I had no clue what she meant."

I responded, "An early April Fools' joke? Are you kidding? Tad, she told me that you kissed her. That was a joke?"

After a moment of silence, he retorted, "And you believed her? So, this was what all the distance has been about. You believing her. Man, this is a trip. Let me get out of here. I don't have time for this junk."

He was even angrier at this point. Tad kept trying to open the door. I was pushing him back. I could not let him go. Simply could not believe that I believed Starr.

Finally, he stopped trying to get out of the restroom and expressed, "You know, you once told me that your girlfriends accused you of something about a pregnancy and never even gave you a chance to explain your side. Well, you are such a hypocrite, 'cause this is basically what you just did to me. You blamed me all this time and never once gave me a chance to clear my name. What were you thinking, anyway? Why would I want to kiss Starr? I struggle to keep from kissing you. Why would it be so easy for me to surrender to someone I barely know?"

"I'm sooo sorry," I cried.

"No babe, sorry doesn't even come close to cutting some of the thickness between us," he replied. "I cared about you so much. It's obvious that you had no faith in me or our relationship. If you did, there is no way you would have believed such trash. And I can't hang with that. We are through."

The next day at Dakari's house, I kept replaying the moment in the bathroom. Although everyone was talking, I only heard Tad's words from yesterday. How could I have been so wrong? Other than shooting the breeze with Hayli about UGA, I was unsociable.

The draft was slowly going by. Drake hadn't gotten picked yet. They were up to the twenty-ninth selection in the first round. Everyone was getting antsy. Already, four linebackers had gone. Mel Kiper, an ESPN draft expert, was predicting Drake to be the next defensive player to go. While they were on edge about that, I was on edge about being such a jerk in my relationship with Tad.

About an hour later, we were all rejoicing as Drake Graham was the second player selected in the second round. Not only were we glad that he went that high, but we were happy that the Atlanta Falcons selected him. It was supposed to be a great fit, with their other linebackers getting older and all.

Dakari took me outside and said, "You know, I've been thinking about what you said earlier. I agree that being happy for Drake doesn't take anything away from me. Believing that made me genuinely enjoy today. I now have confidence that my day will come. Girl, I owe you for your support. With you back in my life, I'm feeling pretty good."

I looked away. Although he was happy, unfortunately, I could not totally share his enthusiasm. I was glad for him and sad for myself. My thoughts were of Tad. The moment I knew I could have Dakari back, I longed for Tad Taylor. I was desperately seeking another chance.

15

Twirling
with Destiny

*P*ayton, I know I don't say this often enough, but I'm
so very proud of you. You have blossomed into a
lovely young lady. Look at you," my mother said proudly as
she stood behind me at the mirror.

It was the day of the debutante ball. The one she had
been waiting for, for a while. My "coming out" night was
finally upon us. Was my mother ready to let go? We
embraced as I noticed a tear trickle down her face.

There were five big dressing areas. A room for the debs,
of course. A place for the escorts. A suite for the mothers. A
corner for the fathers. And a spot for the junior debutantes.

Although our room was supposed to be private, everyone's mother, or in some cases aunts, grandmas, sisters, or
cousins, kept popping in. Some were snapping pictures.
Others were rolling the camcorders. But they all came in at
some point to sneak a peek at our lovely gowns.

The dress was a low-cut, drop-waist, virgin white satin
design with a full flowing skirt. Simple, yet elegant! Covering,

though sexy. Plain, but radiant. Well, if you don't get the picture, maybe I'm not that good at describing it. In other words, we all looked like princesses.

Bare wrists, and fingers. The only jewelry allowed was pearl button earrings and necklace. The Links requested French manicures, and we all complied. At first we thought it wasn't necessary, since we had to wear gloves. Luckily, their wisdom and experience proved that it would make us feel elegant all over.

One thing that troubled me about this whole debutante experience was that we're at the end, and we still weren't as one. I guess girls flocked where they were comfortable. I tried to mix, mingle, and be sociable with as many people as I could. But everyone wasn't as outgoing or friendly.

Some debs were downright cruel. For instance, this lady was standing at the doorway searching for her daughter. I couldn't see who the woman was 'cause my view was blocked. However, I heard girls gossiping and laughing about the woman.

Next, Dymond came up to me and Lynzi in tears. My strong friend was sobbing. How odd to see her weak.

"What's wrong?" I asked.

"Look ya'll," Dy weeped. "They're joking about my mama."

Surely enough, Ms. Johnson was decked out. The twist was, she was dressed very differently than the rest of the mothers. She looked like Halle Berry's sidekick in *Baps*. Big, big, big gold hair. Bright, bright, bright undersized orange gown. Long, long, long fluorescent finger nails. And a gold tooth to top off the attire.

"Ya'lls mamas look so good, so nice, so . . . refined and stuff. My mama look like a ghetto woman. I tried to help her pick somethin' out. She wouldn't let me, though. Said she wanted to surprise me. Now, I'm surprised and embarrassed," Dy sighed.

185

Lynzi then blurted out, "We're over here Mama Johnson."

"Why'd you do that?" Dymond shouted.

"Girl, quit trippin'," Lynzi accused. "Look at my mama. She's suppose to have on a long evening dress. Her version of that is a short miniskirt. My mother is over at the men's side flirting with the dads. Don't you think I'm embarrassed too? But hey, it's my mom! I take her as she is."

Dy responded pitifully, "Yeah, but everyone knows your mama got money. It doesn't matter if she lacks taste. Actually, I can't even believe ya'll wanna be around po' me."

"First of all, you are the strongest, stubbornest, most intelligent gal I know. Do not let this junk get you down and make me have to change my perception of you," I said to her forcefully, yet smiling at the same time. "Girl, we love you for YOU. Not for what you got. Shoot, one day, Ms. Future Doctor, you might make more money than all of us. If that happens, are you gonna drop us from your friend list? Alright then! Besides, we love your mother as well. She has taken good care of us over the years. Mama Johnson feeds us, gives advice, and is sweeter than pie. Ain't none of us ashamed of your mom. And if anybody here has a problem with her, forget 'em. Like Lynzi pointed out, everyone's family has a screw loose somewhere. Besides, a few of these debs don't even have mothers. Chile, be thankful."

She hugged me and uttered, "Thanks! You're right, I am blessed."

It was almost time to line up. Starr sashayed her way over to our group. I hadn't confronted her about her foul little joke. The last thing I wanted was a confrontation, so I ignored her.

But Starr got extremely loud when she picked, "Pay— ton, you never told me how much you liked my early April

Fools' joke. Ha, ha, ha. Did it spoil your relationship? Oh honey, I'm sooo sorry. You believed me, huh? Well, that's probably because it won't be too long before I do get Tad. After all, you ain't giving up nothing. Shucks, there's the real reason why Tad gave you the boot. He is tired of the good girl act."

It had already been a couple of days. Tad had not said anything more than hi. I had apologized over and over. He wasn't trying to hear it. In a sense, Starr was right. He was tired of me. Tired of me asking, begging, and crying for him back. Thinking of all that got me emotional. Plus, Starr pressed other buttons that made me upset.

"What . . . what'd you say?" Starr antagonized. "I'm right!"

Dymond had my back and said, "Look here babe, she don't need to respond to your trifling self. I can't even believe you're acting all tough and bad. I done found out about ya, Missy. You ain't all that. Shooot, Payton might not be givin' it up. But at least she ain't givin' guys venereal diseases like you are."

All our mouths were open. Starr's was too. She seemed shocked.

"That's right. Don't turn red!" Dymond exclaimed. Dakari told Fatz that you gave him gonorrhea. My baby told me not to tell, but now you've pushed me to tell everybody what a slu—nope I'm not gonna go there. I will refrain from calling you the names you are because today I am a debutante. I am too pretty to get ugly. So, while you still have an ounce of dignity, get out of Payton's face. An early April Fools' joke—whoever heard of that anyway? That is so stupid."

We were all lined up and ready to go. The ceremony had begun. I could hear Summer's mother addressing the crowd with the welcome.

It was pretty neat how the event worked. After the welcome and the prayer, we would be introduced one by one. The Civic Center Ballrooms A and B were beautifully decorated with red roses throughout the place.

The guests were seated at round tables of ten. Twenty-five tables were on one side, behind a row of chairs; the same arrangement completed the other side. The dance floor was in the middle. We'd enter through an arch decked with greenery and red roses. Then we would walk down the dance floor with our fathers to the podium, where we debs would sit.

When a name was called, that deb would meet her father under the arch. The mother would then be escorted by the deb's date and present her daughter with a rose and a kiss. Next the escort would seat the mom and walk to the front of the podium and stand.

Of our crew, Dymond was the first to be presented. She was the shortest. Our local TV anchorwoman, Maxi Story, was the commentator for the evening.

Ms. Story stated, "Dymond Johnson is our next lovely debutante. She is being presented by her uncle, given a rose by her mother, and escorted by Mr. Fitzgerald 'Fatz' Coprich. Dymond will attend Howard University, on scholarship, I might add. She plans on becoming a doctor. We hope that after she gets her training, Ms. Johnson will have her practice in Augusta and serve our community with her skills. I'm proud to announce that she has the highest GPA of all our debs this year, with an outstanding 4.0! Dymond's favorite slogan is 'Make the most out of life.' Ladies and gentlemen, I present Ms. Dymond Lashae Johnson."

"You ready, baby?" my father said to me as we stood under the arch. "My little girl is all grown up, and you're the most precious young lady here. I love you."

"Thank you, Daddy. I love you too," I whispered as I

188

squeezed his arm tightly.

"Presenting Miss Payton Skky," the commentator announced. "Payton is a senior at Lucy Laney High School. There she participates in numerous activities. She is also very involved in her church. Payton is unsure as to where she plans to attend college. No . . . wait, I'm receiving a note. Wow, Miss Skky has recently accepted a full four-year scholarship from the University of Georgia. Her career plans are to follow in her father's footsteps and one day own an automobile dealership. She is being presented by her parents, Mr. and Mrs. Paris Skky. Mr. Tad Taylor is her escort this evening. Her favorite motto is 'Wait on the Lord, for only He can take you soaring.' Well, amen. Please give a warm applause to Payton Autumn Skky."

When I sat on the podium, I tried stretching my neck to see Tad's face. I wondered what his reaction was to the news of me going to UGA. A full four-year scholarship—who could turn that down? Plus, it was easy for me to accept it, knowing that Tad was going to be there.

What were his thoughts? I wondered if he was happy about the news. Deep down I was still unsure myself. I realized that a part of my happiness would depend on his response.

"Our next debutante is Miss Starr Love," Ms. Story continued. "Starr is being presented by her parents, the honorable Judge and Mrs. Warren Love. Beautiful Starr is new to our area. However, she has enjoyed her short time at Lucy Laney High School. Currently, she plans to attend a junior college until she determines what her future will hold. She is escorted tonight by Dakari Graham. Her favorite slogan is, 'Carpe diem . . . Seize the day!' Ladies and gents, Miss St—"

The commentator was rudely cut off when an unknown voice shouted, "Miss Tramp!"

I thought that Starr was embarrassed before, when

Dymond called her out. However, that moment couldn't even compete with this one. Starr picked up her dress and sprinted out the side door, as if she were trying to win the forty-yard dash. No one knew what to do. I guess I went off instinct 'cause I got up and trotted after her. I wondered two things: Why was I following Starr, and was my mother going to lose it because I broke protocol?

I found Starr siting in the hallway floor. Her makeup was ruined from tears. God's Spirit had to be at work in me, because my flesh could not give her an ounce of compassion. Yet, the words that flowed from my mouth were only those of kindness, warmth, and help.

"Starr, it's OK," I began as I plopped on the floor next to her.

"You're gonna ruin your dress," she dictated in a caring voice.

"Who cares?" I told her. "That's not even important right now. What is important is you getting up from here and going back in there. We have a ball to finish."

She stumbled, "Nice try, Payton, but . . . I can't waltz back. I'm too humiliated. How could someone say that in front of my parents and—and everybody?"

"People are cruel," I said and turned her face to mine.

"Yeah," Starr stated with her head down, "I deserve that comment. You mean I'm cruel?"

I replied, "I admit you've pulled out a lot of weapons on me this year. I mean, when you took Dakari, it was like a knife in my heart. Your smart comments have been an arrow in my throat, cutting me off and piercing my reply. This latest stunt with Tad was basically a bullet in my head. You had my mind all messed up. To sum it up, you've made this year more than interesting. BUT, it's almost graduation. Time to move on from that pain."

Starr asked humbly, "So are you sayin' you forgive me?"

I thought about it for a second and answered, "Yeah, I

190

guess that's what I'm sayin.'"

"Thank you, Payton. No way do I deserve such mercy. I just don't know if I can face going back in there," Starr responded with caution.

"I can help you face your fears, Starr," we heard a voice say from behind us. "I'll go back in with you."

As we turned, we were both astonished to find Dakari. She ran up to him and squeezed his neck tight. I simply stood and smiled. For the first time, I felt no jealously at the sight of them together. Starr asked us to wait as she went to the ladies' room.

He then came up to me and asserted, "Don't think I want to get back together with her. She's taken me through some things that I can't ignore. But seeing you, of all people, fleeing to her rescue taught me a lot. You showed me how NOT to kick a person when they're down. I care for you so much. Payton, I'm asking once more. Give me another chance?"

Nothing was said for a few seconds. Through all this, I was sure of one thing: Dakari's friendship was starting to mean a great deal to me. I was scared I'd lose it if I let go of his rope of hope. If my response was no, would he be angry, or could we remain friends?

When Dakari noticed I was at a loss for words he continued, "I've got some news for ya. Drake has talked me into not going to Auburn, but being a walk-on at Georgia instead. So, hey, it looks like we're gonna be at the same school. Alright, now I've been waiting on your answer for a while. We've got to get back in there. Before we go, make my night and tell me you'll be mine."

"Come here, big head," I demanded as I gave him a hug. "You're growing into one of my best friends. I'm truly glad to know we'll be at UGA together. We can keep each other straight. But, as far as anything more, I love—"

Before I could get it out, Tad opened the hall door and

saw me locked in Dakari's arms. I pulled loose. Unfortunately, it was too late for explanations. Tad abruptly shook his head in disgust and reentered the cotillion.

"What's up with him?" Dakari asked with concern. "I ain't crazy. I know you sprung on the dude."

I softly said, "Yes, I care deeply for him, but it's over between Tad and me. I wish there was something I could do to change that. So, I've given it to God!"

Starr came out and the three of us went back into the ballroom. Luckily, I sat down just in time to see my girl. Lynzi was walking to the podium.

"Lynzi plans to attend the University of Georgia, where she'll major in psychology. She is being escorted by Mr. Bam Calloway. Presenting Deb Lynzi Meagan Brown," Ms. Story announced.

Boy, was I tired and stiff from sitting in that hard wood chair for an hour. So, I just dazed and thought about the A that Mrs. Armstrong said I was going to receive in physics. The final exam had been an oral presentation. The assignment had been different, but dope. She's such a deep lady. We had to choose an experiment from either Earth science, physical science, biology, chemistry, or physics and relate it to life. Her premise was, there are life lessons in science. She wanted us to find our lesson and tell the class about it.

At first, I didn't give it much thought. However, when Mrs. Armstrong announced that the project would be worth 50 percent of our final grade, I then took it seriously. After much thought, I finally came up with the perfect life science lesson, an analysis on salt.

I took a beaker with a gram of salt and mixed it with one ounce of water. The title was "What happens when you strain a pure substance?" I poured the solution into a petri dish and placed the dish on top of a net. Under the net was a Bunsen burner. It was used to heat the substance. In a minute's time, the water had evaporated. All that was left was a powdery substance comprised of NaCl, also known as sodium chloride. NaCl is salt.

The first question Mrs. Armstrong asked when I completed the experiment was "What type of science test is this?"

"A chemistry project," I quickly replied.

She said with a grin, "Correct. Now, how does this apply to your life?"

I took a deep breath and stated, "Well, basically I have found that when you take a pure substance, salt, and you strain it by diluting the substance and applying heat, in the end, although the substance has changed its physical form, it stays the same pure substance—salt. Now, as far as my life, I'm staying pure as a woman till marriage."

I was interrupted by some jitters. Rude folks. Yes, it was a little awkward to say, but to be true to myself and my experiment, I had to acknowledge that fact.

"Don't laugh, dannng," I admonished. "People, situations, or things have come along and tried to dilute, change, or alter my current state. I've found that although their straining may have made me somehow different, I'm still pure. If pure is what I am . . . if pure is my commitment to myself . . . if pure is my promise to God, then straining me with the temptation of words, muscles, and kisses can't change that."

"Excellent!" Mrs. Armstrong shouted with applause. "You'll receive an A. For the record, I agree with you, Miss Skky. One cannot strain pure to change pure."

"Finally, our last deb," the commentator broke my thoughts and said, "Miss Rain Crandle. Rain is a senior at Lucy Laney High School. There she is captain of the girls' basketball team. In contrast, her favorite hobby is sewing. Rain plans to attend Spelman College. Her life's motto is 'Always give it all you've got.' She is being presented by her parents, Dr. and Mrs. Dwayne Crandle, and her escort is Mr. Tyson Dennis. Ladies and gentlemen, Miss Rain Lynne Crandle. Will you please stand and give a warm 'salute of pride' to all our lovely debs?"

After my mother gave us a charge, we moved on to the fun part of the cotillion. The fun part is the dancing and twirling, the sliding and gliding, the bumping and grind— gotcha! I'm just playin'. This affair was extremely classy.

First we waltzed with our fathers. Then the escorts joined us on the floor as they danced with the mothers. It was tight on the floor 'cause one hundred couples were moving from side to side. Later, the fathers escorted the mothers to their seats. For the remainder of the song, the live jazz band played, and we waltzed with our escorts.

After the waltz, we did a couple other numbers together. Next, the escorts stood aside and we did a deb solo number. That was a blast!

"The Twirl" was the next dance. Everyone looked forward to this complicated fox-trot. There were five big circles, comprised of ten couples. After dancing a few bars with your escort, a deb would then twirl counterclockwise to the next escort. Then twirl again to the next escort. Then twirl again, and keep twirling until she reached her date again.

When I got back to Tad, he viewed me in a special way and uttered, "Payton, you are absolutely beautiful. I probably don't deserve . . . "

I couldn't even hear what he was saying. I was stunned by his warmth. Wasn't he mad at me? Could he possibly be sayin' he still cares?

"Are you listening?" he asked as we glided to the right. "Payton, I'm trying to tell you that I was jealous and angry when I saw you hugging Dakari. I owe you an apology, because just like you did me, I assumed the worst of you. Earlier when Dakari was standing behind me at the podium, he said jokingly that I'd better watch out 'cause he was gonna be doing some huntin.' Huntin' me for the starting job at Georgia and huntin' me for my lady. I thought you guys were getting back together. He told me what was really up."

By this time I was stunned even more. Totally knocked off my feet. I knew Dakari was truly my friend, to have given me up to Tad.

Just as Tad told me this, Dakari winked at me. By this time I was stunned even more. I knew Dakari still liked me. However, despite this fact he did a cool thing. Now Tad had no doubts that I was crazy about him. Dakari was a true friend after all.

At the same time, we said "I love you" to each other. As we slowly walked over to another spot, inside I was elated. Tad was absolutely gorgeous in his black tie and tails. I couldn't believe this was happening. He was so attentive to me and I loved it. I felt just as fresh and vibrant as the budding rose cuddled softly in my hands.

"May I have this dance?" he sweetly asked.

I answered with a warm-filled heart, "Yes you may. No other guy I'd want to dance with."

The moment was wonderful. As he spun me around, things were back to the way I had hoped they would be. Tad, again my man! I felt a sudden peace. God had answered both our prayers. I knew deep in my heart that Tad and I would honor and treasure His gift. We were more than just dancing—we were moving in a glorious triangle with God at the top and Tad and me at each end. We were moving closer to each other as we moved closer to Him. Yep, at that perfect moment we were twirling with destiny.

Other Titles in the Payton Skky Series

Sober Faith

Payton Skky just had the night of her life—introduced to society as a debutante with a bright future, and things were back on track with her new boyfriend and escort, Tad Taylor. However, when it comes time to celebrate, Payton's friends want to toast with something other than punch. Though she wants to be down with her girls, Tad warns her that the consequences could be severe. Which will win...the flesh or the Spirit?

ISBN: 0-8024-4237-4

Saved Race

Payton Skky is about to accomplish a life-long dream—graduate from high school with honors. However, when Payton's gorgeous, biracial, cousin, Pillar Skky steps on the scene and Payton has to deal with feelings of jealousy and anger towards her. Though she knows God wants her to have a tight relationship with her cousin, years of family drama seem to keep them forever apart. Will Payton accept past hurts or embrace God's grace?

ISBN: 0-8024-4238-2

Sweetest Gift

Payton Skky now has what she's always longed for—to go to college and live away from home. Though she quickly finds out that being an adult is not easy. When Payton feels her new friends have it goin'on, she begins to lose self-confidence and starts to feel she doesn't fit in. She can't seem to let go of her sad feelings. Can her relationship with Jesus Christ fill her with joy she lacks?

ISBN: 0-8024-4239-0

Surrendered Heart

ISBN: 0-8024-4240-4

Payton Skky finally has her priorities straight; to live each moment for God. The legacy of her grandfather's life lets her know that in the end the only thing that will matter is knowing for certain that even though people may reject the message of salvation, she still needs to do her best to represent Christ.

Though she gets discouraged, her good friend Tad Taylor helps to keep her focused on carrying out God's commands. While the two of them try to mend their hearts back together, many things around them fall apart. Will they work out...or will things remain the same?

MOODY
PUBLISHERS
THE NAME YOU CAN TRUST.

1-800-678-6928 www.MoodyPublishers.com

STAYING PURE TEAM
============================

ACQUIRING EDITOR
Cynthia Ballenger

COPY EDITOR
Chandra Sparks Taylor

COVER DESIGN
Lydell Jackson

INTERIOR DESIGN
Ragont Design

PRINTING AND BINDING
Versa Press, Inc.

The typeface for the text of this book is
Berkeley